Finding My Father

KAREN HAYES

Orion
Children's Books

First published in Great Britain in 1996
by Orion Children's Books
a division of the Orion Publishing Group Ltd
Orion House
5 Upper St Martin's Lane
London WC2H 9EA

A catalogue record for this book
is available from the British Library

Typeset in Plantin Light by Deltatype Ltd, Ellesmere Port, Cheshire
Printed in Great Britain by Clays Ltd, St Ives plc

ISBN 1 85881 300 X (HB)
ISBN 1 85881 301 8 (PB)

C5 05210499
DB
JF

One

SIMONE COULD FEEL HER HEART THUMPING AS mum sat down at the dinner table and said, 'I've got something to tell you, love.'

Simone had been waiting for this moment for days. She knew her mum had at last made a decision, knew too that she couldn't bear it if the news was bad.

But Mum was smiling. 'France is definitely on,' she said. 'We're off the first day of the school holidays.'

Simone whooped with relief and hugged her mother. 'I'll book a ferry for the first day of the school holidays,' she continued. 'You'll have the whole summer to get to know your grandmother. We owe Grand-mère that.'

Simone couldn't sit still, though she was supposed to be eating her dinner. 'My dad,' she said passionately. 'At last, I'll see where he was born, where he grew up.'

'And I can show you where he and I met.' Mum said this softly, her eyes thoughtful.

Simone was so keyed up she could hardly finish her meal, even though Mum made the best lasagne in Devon. All she wanted to do was to talk about France. She and Mum gave up trying to eat as they chatted non-stop about the trip, about Grand-mère, about her father. They cleared the table, did the washing up, and still Simone kept making plans. It was an hour later when, reluctantly, she finally left Mum to mark some papers while she went upstairs to her bedroom.

She had some English homework which she knew she ought to be writing, but she couldn't, just couldn't. She had waited so long for this that she wasn't about to spoil it with schoolwork. Flopping down on the red duvet on her bed, she stared at her poster of King Arthur and the Knights of the Round Table, splendid in their armour. On the shelf beneath the poster were Simone's books about Camelot. And next to them was a faded photograph of her father, Jean-Claude, taken when he was a boy a few years younger than Simone was now. Jean-Claude was holding a long cardboard sword covered with silver paper, lifting it with both hands over his head as though it was some incredible trophy.

'He made that sword himself, called it Excalibur,' Mum had told Simone. 'Your father loved the tales of King Arthur and Sir Lancelot and Merlin the Wizard and the others when he was young.' Soon after this, Mum had given Simone a book about Camelot, which she had read so many times the pages were beginning to tear. She had read the others avidly too. It made her feel close to her father.

Downstairs, she could hear Mum talking to someone and knew that Billy had arrived. Billy was Mum's friend – her boyfriend, Simone's friend Angie called him, because he was always taking Mum out to dinner, or to the art cinema to see foreign films. Mum was a widow, though that seemed an odd word for someone who looked so young, with her long dark hair, her tiny slim figure. Simone's father had been killed in a car accident a month before she was born.

Jean-Claude was French, he came from a small village in Brittany where Grand-mère still lived. There was a large photo of him in a plain wooden frame in the living room, taken just before he died. He looked young and happy, with flyaway curly hair and a big toothy grin. Simone had inherited both the flyaway hair, which she didn't mind because it was a rich red-gold colour like her father's, and the toothy grin, which she hated but couldn't do much about. Mum said her smile was endearing and made people want to smile back, but Mum was always saying things like that, as if trying to compensate for her not having a father, nor any brothers or sisters.

'Don't you ever get lonely?' Angie had once asked. 'Just you and your mum, living on your own?' Angie came from a huge family, three brothers and a sister as well as a mum and dad.

'I've never noticed if I do,' Simone had replied thoughtfully. 'Mum is always there when I get home from school, and in the holidays we do lots of things together.'

Simone's mum was a teacher, at the same comprehensive school Simone went to. She taught French, which was how she had met Simone's father. She was taking her first school trip to France with some GCSE students, to a town in Brittany called Pontivy. Jean-Claude was an English teacher at the school they exchanged with, so Mum saw him again not many months later when the French students came over to Exeter on a return visit. By the end of the year Jean-Claude had not only married the young English woman, but had moved to Exeter where he soon got a job teaching French at the college.

'It's such a romantic story,' Angie had sighed, whenever she thought about Simone's mum and dad.

'You keep saying that,' Simone groaned the last time Angie had brought it up. 'But it didn't end romantically, did it? They'd only been married two years when my dad had the car crash.'

'Lots of romantic stories have tragic endings. Look at Romeo and Juliet, or Sir Lancelot and Guinevere.'

Simone gave up. Angie was a dreamer. Simone had told her a hundred times how hard it was for Mum, raising her on her own, having to hold down a tough job as well as look after a baby, then a young child.

But all Angie could see was a handsome Frenchman and a beautiful English girl meeting and falling in love and marrying within a year. And to be honest, sometimes when Simone was feeling low and wondering what it would have been like to have had a father, she too would dream about the good bits, her mum and dad happy, planning to have children, planning to have *her*.

Looking at the photo of Jean-Claude, Simone felt a rush of love for the father she had never known or seen. Mum had, of course, told her all about him, so that she had grown up feeling as though he was a vital if invisible part of the household. Sometimes she felt she was closer to her dead father than a lot of her friends were to their living, breathing fathers.

And now she was going to meet his mother – her grandmother – for the very first time. She felt prickly with anticipation. Through Grand-mère, her father would become even more real, more alive to her, than he was now. The thought so overwhelmed her that she jumped up from the bed and took a photograph album from her shelves, leafing through the pages quickly and stopping at her favourite photograph. It was of her father as a young man, standing outside an old stone cottage, on his way (Mum had told her) to college where he would be trained as a teacher.

Simone stared at the photo, though she knew it by

heart. Her father had grown up in that small stone house, and Grand-mère was still living there. Soon, she would be there too. Closing the album quickly as shivers of excitement ran up and down her spine, Simone flopped back on the bed again, her homework forgotten. What would Jean-Claude's home be like? What would Grand-mère be like?

Mixed with the exhilaration, she felt unease. What would Grand-mère think of *her*, Simone – her only grandchild, and a half English one at that? Would she understand Simone's French? Would she approve of her English ways? What was she expecting of Simone, the only child of her only son?

Downstairs Mum and Billy were laughing. Simone could hear the rumble of their voices, but not what they were saying. Simone liked Billy, even though she wished Mum would call him Bill – Billy sounded like someone's little brother. But apart from his name, Simone hadn't minded the way he had casually entered their lives about six months ago, hanging around in the evenings, and at least one day of the week-end. To be honest, she *had* resented him to start with, but Billy was easy-going and relaxed and eager to please, rather like an overgrown sheepdog, and soon he had won her over.

'How romantic!' Angie had sighed when Billy first came upon the scene.

'Oh yeah,' Simone had muttered sarcastically. 'A bearded, short-sighted *teacher* of all things, cooking shepherd's pie in the kitchen. That's really romantic.'

'He's always around these days. I can't remember anyone hanging around here like Mr Sanders does.'

Simone cringed. 'Mr Sanders, my biology teacher. And he said I should call him Billy at home – can you imagine? Yuk!'

'You always liked him!' Angie practically shouted.

'Well, I suppose, but only in class. I'm not sure I like him here all the time.'

But in the end she didn't mind. Though she still found it hard to call him Billy . . .

A few weeks later, Billy was standing on the pier in Plymouth waving good-bye to Simone and her mum as the ferry chugged towards France.

'*Au revoir!*' Mum was shouting.

When Billy was almost out of sight, Mum put her arm around Simone's shoulder and said lightly, 'I'll miss him.'

Simone was too thrilled to be on the boat at last, heading towards her father's home, to think about Billy. 'We'll have Grand-mère for company,' she said.

Mum was quiet. The sea was flat and shiny, like a deep blue-grey mirror, and the early morning sun shone over it, promising fine weather. Finally she said, in French, 'You must be understanding with Grand-mère, Simone. For a start, she's much older than your other grandmother. She had your father when she was over forty, and he was her only child. Now that Grand-père is dead, we are her only family.'

Mum often spoke in French to Simone, 'so you never forget that you are half French.' Mum spoke it perfectly, and so did Simone, for when Jean-Claude died, Mum made sure that his only child knew his language even before learning English. In primary school Simone had often been ashamed of the way she spoke English with a slight French accent, as if she were a foreigner. But now that everyone was required to take French at school, she was proud that she could speak and understand so well.

But a whole summer of speaking nothing but French? Simone was hit by an unexpected attack of anxiety. She knew that none of the locals in the tiny isolated village where Grand-mère lived spoke English. Would she cope?

Mum, reading her thoughts, hugged her quickly and said, 'You'll be fine, just fine. Come on, let's go inside and get a hot chocolate and a *pain aux raisin*. We're on a French boat, so let's start eating French food.'

Cheered up again, Simone followed Mum. Suddenly, she couldn't wait to get to Brittany, to meet her long-lost grandmother and to see her father's home for herself at last.

The rain was thundering down when they finally reached the little village of Kerlennec. It was Monday and everything was closed: the *boulangerie*, the tiny grocery store, the small *charcuterie*. The bar was open, but looking in through the windows as they drove by, Simone saw that it was empty. It looked grim and dreary, like the village itself in the rain. Not even the huge stone church in the middle of the square looked welcoming. There was no sign of life anywhere.

Grand-mère lived about two kilometres outside the village. Her house was very old, made of grey stone with pale blue faded shutters on all the windows. It was one of a cluster of four or five buildings: a small farm hamlet, Mum said. It was called *Truez-er Lann*, which Mum tried to translate for Simone from the ancient Breton language to the French.

'I think *truez* means *triste*, which means sad in French. *Lann* means some kind of moorland.'

'So we're staying at some place called "Sad on the Moor,"' Simone murmured. She decided she'd write this in a letter to Angie tomorrow. Angie would find it romantic and mysterious, like she did most things.

They had approached Truez-er Lann and Mum was slowing down the car. The cluster of houses seemed to be in the middle of nowhere. There were some hills and woods, some drenched cows and a flat wet field, but no moor that Simone could see.

Simone noticed that some of the crumbling stone buildings were houses – you could tell by the shutters and by the smoke coming from the chimneys – and the others were barns. A solitary dog howled forlornly as they drove up, but Simone saw no sign of it.

Mum parked the estate car at the back of the house, alongside the cobbled courtyard. Red geraniums bloomed in clay pots along some steep stone steps at the side of the house.

'Well, here we are!' Mum said brightly, but Simone could see she was close to tears. 'It's not changed much since I was here.'

Mum had only visited Grand-mère once, when she and Jean-Claude (Simone often thought of him as Jean-Claude, instead of 'Dad') were first married, when Grand-père was alive. Grand-père was old even then, much older than Grand-mère, and very set in his ways. He hadn't wanted his only son to marry an Englishwoman and move so far away, and though he was polite and welcoming, he could not hide his bitterness from Jean-Claude. Before the visit was over, the two men had had a terrible row. Grand-père said he never wanted to set eyes on Jean-Claude again.

'And he never did,' Mum had said sadly, years later. 'Grand-mère and I tried to get the two men to make up their foolish quarrel, but both your father and grandfather were stubborn and neither of them would make the first move.'

Mum had hoped that when her baby was born, Grand-père would relent and they would all three go to Brittany for a joyful reunion. But instead, Jean-Claude was killed, and Grand-père, mad with grief, refused to see or even speak about his son's wife and child ever again.

Now Grand-père too was dead, and Simone was about to meet her grandmother for the first time. She knew from photographs that she would not be like her other granny, who looked like one of the models she photographed for the fashion magazine she worked for. Simone liked visiting her mum's mother in London, staying at her small elegant flat, going out shopping or to lunch at new restaurants.

But she wasn't prepared for how strange Grand-mère *did* look. The door of the house opened, and Simone could see a tall stern-looking woman with pure white hair and a face as wrinkled as a crumpled page in an exercise book. '*Belle-mère*,' Mum said, getting out of the car and going to her.

Simone knew that *belle-mère* was the French word for mother-in-law, but she couldn't understand a word of what Grand-mère said to Mum, for she spoke with a heavy Breton accent. Simone watched as the two adults embraced, and cried. It made Simone want to cry too, though she didn't know why.

When they pulled apart, Mum called Simone over. Simone was reluctant to leave the car somehow. It seemed safe and reassuring, while the old stone house loomed cold and strange.

But she got out and walked over to her new grandmother. 'My son's child, come home at last,'

Grand-mère said in unrecognizable French, and cried some more, and clung to Simone even harder than she did to Mum.

Simone felt stiff and uncomfortable in her arms. She was dismayed to find that this foreign woman was a stranger to her; somehow she had expected to feel as close to her as she felt to her father, even though she had never known either of them.

Grand-mère looked like no one she had ever seen before. She wore a quaint black dress which fell to her ankles, and over it a white lacy apron. On her head perched a funny cap which looked like an upside down mug. It was called a *coiffe*, made of exquisite fine lace. Mum explained later that this was the traditional costume for Breton women. Grand-mère was very old and still dressed formally for special occasions.

They finally got inside the house. There was one big room downstairs which seemed to be both a living room and a kitchen, with an old-fashioned stone sink in the corner next to an ancient wood-burning cooker and stove. A battered sofa which looked like it could seat six people was pushed against the far wall, and near the stove there was a long plain wooden table with narrow benches on either side.

The room was dark, despite the glow of the fire in the stove. It seemed shabby and worn, though it was spotlessly clean. Simone had been to France often before, camping on the beaches with Mum, but this was something else. She didn't mind shabbiness – their own house in England certainly wasn't luxurious – but there was a depressing feel to the place, as if years of sadness had made the air itself heavy and dark.

But Grand-mère had taken her hand and was leading her to the long oak table. Simone saw that it was covered with food, fresh and beautifully laid out: a large ham, prawns, salads, bread rolls, various cheeses.

Simone sat down to eat. Though the food looked delicious and she was hungry, she felt close to tears. She could hardly understand Grand-mère's French, nor her odd formal manner, even though the old woman seemed pleased to see her. And Grand-mère didn't look at all like her father, not from the photographs she had seen.

The rain, beating heavily on the roof, made a dreary dull rhythm. Simone shivered, feeling damp and cold. The wood stove smouldered, making her eyes water. Grand-mère, sitting unsmiling at the top of the table, was looking at her solemnly. It made Simone feel awkward.

Suddenly, the summer she had been so looking forward to seemed to loom ahead as something shaky and uncertain. Where was her father? Simone thought with despair. Where was Jean-Claude whom she was hoping to find here?

Trying to hide her dismay from Mum and Grand-mère, Simone picked up her fork and knife and, with difficulty, because her appetite was gone, she began to eat.

Two

SIMONE WAS DREAMIMG OF A YOUNG FRENCH boy with red-gold hair and a toothy grin when the sun woke her up next morning.

'This used to be your father's bedroom,' Grand-mère had told her as she showed Simone upstairs, kissing her twice on each cheek as she bade her good-night. Simone had stiffened at the kiss, and could not bring herself to respond. She knew the old woman was family, and the only relative she had on her father's side, but to Simone, Grand-mère was about as family as an alien from space.

But she loved the idea of sleeping in Jean-Claude's room. Last night as she had looked around the small bedroom, at the bookshelves full of her father's old books and trinkets, the yellowing posters of King Arthur on the walls, Simone felt she had never been so close to him. It made everything else seem worthwhile – the gloomy house, her stern grandmother. She unpacked her bags feeling Jean-Claude's presence as she had never felt it before: loving, caring, enveloping her with his strength and affection.

The feeling had persisted as she lay awake in bed, the same bed that her father had slept in as a child. As she drifted off to sleep, she could see his face, clearer than any photograph. She felt that she could reach out and touch him. Although it was only a dream, the next morning she still had a powerful sense of his presence. It made her happy, for it was as if he needed her as much as she needed him.

Simone got out of bed, opened the shutters and looked out of the window. Was this what her father saw, the first thing every morning, when *he* was her age? The blackbird sitting in the old gnarled willow tree in front of the house? The barn looking like it was made of ancient gold stones, with the sun shining on it like this?

Simone couldn't tear herself away from the window. The sunlight and clear blue sky made everything look different this morning. The cottage opposite had pink roses growing up its front wall, and there were daisies and marigolds everywhere.

A frail stooped man with a dark flat cotton cap looked up and waved, and she waved uncertainly back. A mongrel dog that looked like a black bear cub, barked good-naturedly up at her. '*Bonjour, mademoiselle,*' the man said and wandered off towards the barn.

Grand-mère and Mum were in the kitchen when Simone came down. The sun had brightened up this room like everything else: it had miraculously turned cheery.

Simone kissed her mum but avoided Grand-mère's kiss by ducking her head. Though her grandmother was no longer wearing the lacy *coiffe* and apron, she still looked strange and forbidding. She wore a severe brown dress of some coarse material, with long sleeves even though the morning was already quite warm. She had on thick black stockings and wooden clogs. Mum said they were called *sabots* and that all the Breton people wore them years ago, and many still did.

Grand-mère took off her clogs at the door, leaving on the shapeless felt slippers she wore inside them.

Her white hair must have been very long, because it was wrapped around and around her head in a thick coil, like a fat snake. She looked like a witch, Simone thought, and then felt guilty because Grand-mère was smiling at her and offering her sweet black coffee and a croissant.

Simone took the coffee, in spite of Mum trying to get her to drink milk instead, and tried to smile back at Grand-mère but she found it hard-going.

'So like Jean-Claude,' the old woman muttered as she stared at Simone, her eyes filling with tears.

Embarrassed, Simone hastily ate her croissant and said she was going out to explore. Outside, the sun was already hot and bright, making up for the miserable day yesterday. Simone had to admit that things looked much better. the geraniums redder, pinker, perkier; the cobbled courtyard dazzling in the morning light. It still looked lonely though. The cluster of stone buildings had been part of a farm for centuries, but now only the old people were left, the ones who were children when the farm still *was* a farm. The old man she had seen earlier had disappeared into the barn opposite, which had been turned into a makeshift cottage, and even the dog had vanished.

Simone, feeling as if she had stumbled upon a ghost town, wandered through an archway of green shrubbery at the back of her grandmother's house and found herself in a tiny garden, full of hydrangea bushes with jaunty blue flowers. An enormous apple tree was in the corner, and as Simone went up to see if the fruit was ripe yet, she heard an eerie sound coming from the upper branches.

It took a moment for her to realize that it was a human sound – the sound of laughter, but peculiar laughter, like someone hiccuping. Then there was a sound of rustling leaves, and a slight figure slid down the trunk and landed in a heap in front of her.

'*Bonjour*,' the surprising figure said, and then carried on in a torrent of French that Simone didn't understand, it was so heavily accented.

'Please, speak more slowly,' Simone said in her best French. She was disconcerted when the boy, for that's what it was, began to laugh again.

He was probably Simone's age, but was much smaller and thinner. He had straight ebony hair that was all in a tangle, and beautiful olive skin with large elf-like eyes. The bizarre thing about him was the way he was dressed, in long, thick raggedy black trousers, and a prim but grubby white shirt which looked like something an old man would wear.

The boy giggled again, then clapped both hands to his mouth like a mischievous child, cutting off his own laughter. His eyes widened in mock horror: Simone couldn't decide whether it was at her French, or his own senseless fit of giggles. Before she could decide what to do next, the boy said something else, but again Simone could not understand.

'*Pardon?*' Simone said. '*Je ne comprends pas.*'

He looked at her so sadly that Simone was startled, wondering if he had totally misunderstood her. Then, with dignity, he turned and ran from the garden.

'Did you meet any of our neighbours?' Grand-mère asked Simone later, as they sat down to a lunch of crêpes that Grand-mère had made in a big round iron skillet on the wood-stove.

Simone was getting used to her grandmother's accent now so she was able to reply, 'I saw a boy in the garden, but I couldn't understand what he was saying.'

Grand-mère chuckled, and her face wrinkled up like a crumpled tissue. One of her front teeth was crooked. 'That's André. He's the grandson of Monsieur Arragon, who used to farm the land around here. He lives in the cottaage opposite. André's father is Spanish and he speaks French with a Basque accent. You'll soon get used to it.'

'How nice,' Mum said brightly. 'A friend for you.'

Oh, brilliant, Simone thought. A friend who giggles like an idiot, who doesn't understand a word I say, and who dresses like a real weirdo and hangs out in apple trees.

She rolled her eyes at her mother, but nonetheless she was intrigued by their odd neighbour. After lunch she wandered outside but the small hamlet was deserted, so she went up to her room.

As soon as she had shut herself in the tiny bedroom, she felt her father around her once again and promptly forgot about the boy. Contentedly, she began looking through the shelves, at one or two toys and games that used to belong to Jean-Claude. There was a Dominoes set, a bag of marbles, and a carved wooden statue that seemed to be of an old man with a long beard and a funny tall hat, like a wizard.

Reverently, Simone picked up the books, which were yellow and musty. She leafed through them and found one about the Knights of the Round Table. As Simone turned the pages, she imagined her father as a boy lying in this same bed, looking at the Camelot book as she looked at hers back home. The thought made her tingle with pleasure.

A shout from beneath her window startled her. Opening the blue shutter which she had closed to keep out the glare of the sun, Simone saw André grinning up at her.

She still couldn't understand much of what he said, but he had a tennis ball in his hand. Next to him the big black bear cub of a dog was leaping about trying to get the ball. Simone understood that André wanted to get her to come outside and play.

She hesitated. André seemed so crazy, jumping up and down with the ball like there were ants crawling up his trousers, while the dog barked frantically at his feet. But the sun was shining enticingly outside.

She joined André in the cobbled square separating Grand-mère's house from the other buildings. He threw the ball to Simone who threw it to the dog, who was called Cassis.

'What a funny name for a dog,' Simone said.

To her surprise, André understood her French this time. 'I named him after my favourite blackcurrant ice-cream. It's a good name, *n'est-ce pas?*'

By now, Simone was beginning to make sense of André's unfamiliar accent. When he realized this, he became quite talkative.

'My mother said it was a stupid name, but I don't care. She never sees Cassis anyway.'

'I don't understand,' Simone said.

André shrugged. 'Mama works in a café in Paris, and Papa is a sailor. There is no work here, you see.'

'When do you see them?' Simone asked curiously.

André looked down at his feet, tucking his chin into his chest then gazing sideways at Simone as if sizing her up. He looked exactly like an elf, Simone thought.

'Mama comes to Brittany when she can have some time off from work. She says Paris is not a good place for children, not where she lives. Papa comes when he is home from the sea, but it is a long way. His boat is docked in Spain. He is Spanish, you see. They both see me whenever they can.'

André said this last sentence defiantly, as if challenging Simone to contradict him. But she said nothing, and the defiance gave way to the same look of sadness Simone had seen earlier. He looked like a lost little boy now.

Simone didn't know what to say. Suddenly André began jumping up and down like a maniac, exciting Cassis who barked and ran around in circles. André threw the ball to Simone, who threw it for Cassis.

'Are you here on holiday?' Simone asked, when it looked like André was not going to offer any more information. 'Will you go back to Paris when the summer holidays are over?'

He tossed his head and grimaced, as if Simone were a stupid child who had to have everything spelt out. His teeth were very white in his olive face. '*Mais non!*' he explained. 'I told you Mama doesn't think children should be raised in Paris, No, no, no, I live here.' He pointed to the stone cottage opposite, where Monsieur Arragon lived.

As they turned towards the house, the brown door opened and Simone recognized the old man who had waved to her that morning.

'My grandpa,' André said proudly. He ran up to the frail, bent man, grabbed him by the hand, and pulled him towards Simone. '*Enchanté*,' Monsieur Arragon said, shaking Simone's hand. She noticed that he too was wearing heavy wooden clogs, like Grand-mère.

André was so excited that he was running madly around and around, like Cassis had done earlier. Simone thought that life in this place must be very dull indeed if this bit of socializing could get him so wound up. The dog jumped up at him, yapping hysterically. His grandfather just smiled.

Grand-mère and Mum, hearing the noise, came out into the front garden. Grand-mère introduced Mum to Monsieur Arragon, and there were tears in her eyes again as she explained who Mum was, and who Simone was. Monsieur Arragon looked as if he were going to weep as well. He kept holding Simone's hand and saying, 'Ah, Jean-Claude's daughter, ah, ah! Jean-Claude's child, home at last.'

Simone turned away. For a moment she felt both angry and confused. Close as she felt to her father here, it was her secret, and she wanted to keep it herself, hide it where no one could see it. And here were these old people, shouting it out to all the world.

André saw her look away and clutched her elbow. 'Come on, I'll beat you to the apple tree,' he shouted, and raced across the courtyard and around the house, towards the back garden.

'Come on!' he shouted. Cassis barked furiously.

'Go on,' Mum said. 'He's got a good head start.'

Simone was so relieved to get away from the grown-ups that even with his head start, she almost beat André.

'Here, come up the tree,' he said, giggling his hiccuping laugh. 'There's plenty of room for two on this branch.'

It was a thick strong branch, quite high up, wide enough to sit on comfortably. As they settled in the tree, André became quiet and broody. Simone, not yet used to his swift changes of mood, wondered what was wrong. Finally he said, 'Are you coming to live with your Grand-mère? Like I live with Grand-père?'

'NO!' The word came out so explosively that André was startled.

'No,' Simone said more calmly. 'My mother and I are here just for the summer.'

André didn't reply. He looked thoughtful, and wistful, too. Older as well – no longer a little child. Not looking at Simone, he stared out between the thick branches of the apple tree.

Simone wondered when André had last seen his parents, wondered what it was like living in this isolated spot all year long with no one but a very old man for company. She was glad she had her mum, and even her dad, though she knew André would think her crazy if she said that aloud. Jean-Claude might be dead, but Simone thought he seemed more alive here at Truez-er Lann than André's living, faraway father.

Although it drizzled the next few days, Simone didn't mind. She explored the house and derelict barns surrounding it. She imagined Jean-Claude doing his homework at the solid, scarred desk in the living room, or helping his father sort apples in the storeroom.

When the rain stopped, Simone and Mum walked to the village of Kerlennec. They had a delicious hot chocolate in the café.

'Ah, Jean-Claude's daughter!' the owners exclaimed. Other customers crowded around, introducing themselves.

'I remember Jean-Claude well,' said a skinny man with a beard.

'He was such a quiet boy,' chimed in another, fatter man.

'I was with him at school,' a woman interrupted. 'His head always in a book. Is his daughter like him?'

They went on like this for ages. Mum went all funny, sort of teary and happy and proud and sad, all at the same time. At first Simone was shattered, as if someone had ripped something precious out of her and passed it around like slices of birthday cake. But gradually, as the villagers fussed over them, and reminisced about Jean-Claude, she was overcome by a strong pride. She felt as if she were taking her place at his side, in his village, with his people.

The feeling persisted as they left Kerlennec. As they trudged up the hill towards home, Simone saw two girls around her age cycling past. They waved in a friendly manner, and Mum and Simone waved back. One of them, in jeans and a T-shirt, reminded Simone of Angie.

One hot clear afternoon, Mum drove Simone to Pontivy, a town about twenty miles away. Grand-mère said she didn't want to go, and Simone was glad. She still felt very awkward around that strange woman, with her long dark dresses, her wooden clogs, her hair like a white snake. She couldn't believe Grand-mère was Jean-Claude's mother.

'I wish I could get your grandmother out and about a bit,' Mum said as they sat outside under an umbrella, drinking Orangina. It had got hot again, and they had decided to have a cool drink before exploring the town.

'What does she do all day?' Simone asked. 'She doesn't have a car. How does she get to the village for food?'

Mum took a sip of her drink. 'Believe it or not, Grand-mère only gave up cycling a year or so ago, when her hip became stiff with arthritis. She used to cycle back and forth to the village for her bread and provisions. Now Monsieur Arragon shops for her. Since Grand-père died, she has become something of a recluse, hardly ever leaves the house. It worries me.'

'Is that old bike hers? The one in the back shed?'

'Yes. She said you could use it if you like.'

'It's a hundred years old!'

Mum smiled. 'Not quite. Have a go sometime.'

Simone thought of the two girls she had seen in Kerlennec, on their shiny new mountain bikes, and decided she'd be the laughing stock of the village if she cycled into Kerlennec on Grand-mère's ancient bike. She'd stick to walking, thank you.

Mum seemed to be in a trance in Pontivy. She had met her husband, Jean-Claude here, and had only been back once since.

'We sat up there, on the grass in front of the château,' Mum said.

They walked up to the castle, which was massive and forbidding, with its grey and black stone walls and its vast round tower. Sitting on the grass, Mum told Simone the story again of how she and Jean-Claude met.

'We had taken our English students here, on a day's outing. We had all brought sandwiches and were eating on this very spot, waiting for the French pupils and their teachers to show up. They were meeting us here, you see.'

Simone closed her eyes, picturing it. The great castle looming in the background, the shade of the poplar trees in front, the warm lazy spring day. Then the noisy, excited arrival of the French kids, mingling with the shouts of the English children. And Jean-Claude, her father, suddenly *here*, introducing himself to Mum, sitting next to her, laughing and tossing his red-gold hair as she offered him half of her sandwich . . .

It was a nice memory, though Simone realized it wasn't *her* memory but her mother's. Being here now, she felt it was hers too. How good it was, to be in her father's country, to be with his people.

Mum showed her other places, too. The café where she and Jean-Claude had sat for an hour when the students were free to explore the town – it was still there, much to Mum's delight. And so was the flower stall on the corner of a back street, where he had bought her a bouquet of fresh spring flowers.

They were both in a quiet mood when they got home. The first thing they saw was Grand-mère, in the courtyard, sweeping the stone cobbles with an old-fashioned broom. All Simone's and Mum's clothes were hung out on the line.

'Belle-mère, you didn't need to do that!' Mum cried.

Grand-mère smiled, showing her crooked tooth. 'It is good for me to work, to have something to do. My life has a purpose now, a meaning.'

'Her life must be pretty pathetic if the only meaning she can find in it is hand-washing all our dirty clothes,' Simone muttered in English.

Mum turned to her and frowned. 'You must never think your grandmother pathetic,' she replied in English. 'She has worked hard all her life, and that work has given her life dignity and purpose. It's not something to sneer at.'

Simone was stung at the anger in Mum's voice. She hadn't meant to be rude; the words just came out. Why couldn't Mum understand that, understand how *she* felt instead of taking Grand-mère's side? Dismayed, she disappeared to her room.

Once there, she was comforted. It was as if Jean-Claude were still in the room, looking after her, understanding her confusion over this alien place, her conflicting feelings about his peculiar mother. Simone couldn't get used to Grand-mère, couldn't warm towards her. Even though her mum didn't see this, she knew her dad did. If he were alive he'd explain things to Mum, tell her how hard it was for Simone.

But he's not alive. Shaking that thought from her head, Simone left the room and headed for the enclosed garden, to see if André was in the apple tree. He was.

'Do you live up there?' she shouted.

'I *think* up here,' André replied seriously.

He was like that. One minute he acted years younger than his age, the next he was talking like a grown-up.

Simone followed him up into the tree, and sat back on the sturdy branch. Underneath, Cassis barked, frustrated because she couldn't climb up with them.

André was withdrawn, preoccupied. On the top branch a blackbird sang, unafraid of the two intruders.

'Sometimes I make up stories,' André said all of a sudden, in a secretive, confiding manner. 'Maybe I'll tell you one sometime. They're very good.'

Simone didn't answer. She could think of better things to do than listen to André telling stories in the apple tree.

'What do you do in the winter?' Simone asked, to change the subject. 'When it's too wet and cold to sit in the apple tree?'

André thought about this, frowning. 'There's school, of course,' he said finally. 'And I play Dominoes with Grand-père.' He never even mentioned seeing his parents.

It sounded awful to Simone. André lapsed into a brooding silence. Simone, wishing she hadn't come outside, narrowed her eyes and tried to imagine Jean-Claude in this same tree, sitting on the same gnarled branch. But all she could see was André, small and slight and unusually still, gazing out beyond the leaves to some world of his own.

Simone shivered. Without a word of explanation, she climbed down past André and hurried back to the house, to her bedroom where she could once again feel Jean-Claude's spirit wrapping around her like a soft warm cloak, embracing and protecting her.

André hardly noticed her leaving. When Simone looked back at the apple tree, he was still staring at the sky, frozen by whatever it was he was seeing.

Simone spent much of the next week with André. Though he often annoyed her with his silliness, his terrible giggles and manic behaviour, he could also be sensible and fun. Just when he drove her so mad she never wanted to see him again, he could completely change. He knew interesting bits of history, old Breton legends, and wove fascinating games and stories around them.

She was also glad that someone her age was around. All the other occupants of the hamlet were old, and she hadn't seen the two girls from Kerlennec again. She thought again of André, isolated here with nothing but wrinkled, white-haired people, and shuddered.

Mum, on the other hand, didn't seem to mind that there was no one her age to talk to, that she was stuck all day with Grand-mère. 'Aren't you bored here?' Simone had asked her once, when Mum was sitting in the courtyard with Grand-mère, who was crocheting an intricate pattern of lace.

Mum was writing a letter to Billy, which she seemed to do every day. She frowned slightly at Simone's use of English. She had told Simone it was rude in front of

Grand-mère, who couldn't understand a word of it. Simone kept forgetting. She wished Mum would remember how hard it was to talk in a foreign language all the time, no matter how well you knew it. Where Grand-mère was concerned, Mum wasn't very understanding these days.

Mum answered, in French, of course, 'I love the Brittany countryside. Our walks to the village, sitting in the garden with Belle-mère – I find it very peaceful after the stress of teaching.'

Grand-mère looked fondly at her. 'Jean-Claude missed the tranquillity here, when he went off to college. He said he always loved coming home for the holidays.'

The two women exchanged warm looks, as they always did when they were talking about Jean-Claude. Mum said, dreamily. 'When I knew I was pregnant, Jean-Claude talked of moving to the country. We were so happy, then. He wanted a daughter, you know.'

Simone liked to listen to them talk. She could feel him taking shape as a real father, not just the fantasy one she had imagined in England.

One hot sunny day, Mum drove Simone and André to a lake, about ten kilometres away. It was a brilliant place. The lake was vast, with forests all around, but with a sandy beach on one shore. It was great for swimming, and there were paddleboats too, which were quite cheap to rent by the hour.

Grand-mère as usual stayed home, cooking and cleaning and sitting out amongst her geraniums. When they got to the lake, Mum spread a blanket on the grass above the sand, pulled out a paperback and settled down to read.

André was beside himself with excitement, acting like a dummy again. He was waving his arms and shouting with glee, causing other people to stare and then smile.

'You act like you've never been here before,' Simone said crossly. She was cross because she was mortified. Not far from them, in swimming costumes, were the two girls from the village. They were looking at André and smirking.

André was pulling off his black trousers, to reveal an equally ridiculous swimming costume. It was black too, and looked as if it were made of wool, it seemed so thick and heavy. It drooped to his skinny knees, but he didn't seem to mind. He was hopping from one foot to the other, telling Simone to hurry up and change.

Simone realized that André probably rarely came here. His grandfather had a fossilized Citröen that just about made it to the village and back. She couldn't imagine Monsieur Arragon and André out picnicking at the lake, somehow.

'Come on, let's try the water,' she said, trying to avoid the staring eyes of the two girls.

'Wait a minute. Put on some sun cream first,' Mum said. 'That sun is hot. You don't want to burn.'

André looked bewildered, but let Mum rub cream on his back. Then they ran down to the water and waded in, until they were up to their shoulders.

'Hmm, wonderful,' Simone said.

André couldn't swim, but he was happy enough to paddle about while Simone practised her breast stroke. Every once in a while he let out a delirious whoop, causing the swimmers nearby to turn and stare.

When they came out of the water, Mum gave them some francs to buy ice-cream at the café at the end of the lake. 'You have to have a *cassis* ice-cream,' André ordered. 'Blackcurrant. It's the best, it's fabulous, *c'est formidable!*'

'It – is – the – best,' Simone said slowly in English, trying to get André to repeat it. She was trying to teach him some English. To her surprise, he was quite a good student. 'Zee best,' he repeated. 'Eet ees zee best.'

'Well done,' Simone smiled. André rolled his big eyes and pulled monkey faces to show how clever he was.

They got their ice creams and sat at a table outside, in the shade of a willow tree. While they were eating, the girl from Kerlennec who reminded Simone of Angie stopped by their table. Her friend was with her.

'Good afternoon, miss,' the Angie look-alike said in pompous, stilted English. Both girls giggled.

Simone stiffened. She felt she was being made fun of. She was more than ever aware that she was an outsider in their close-knit little village.

But the other girl, the blonde one with frizzed hair, smiled kindly and said, in French, 'You speak excellent French. We heard you talking to André.'

The one who was dark and plump, like Angie, said wistfully, 'I wish my English was as good as your French.'

'Me too,' said the blonde. 'My teacher at school says I am hopeless.'

Simone realized that they weren't making fun at all. Relief washed over her like a clean shower of rain after a hot sticky day.

They began to talk. The dark girl was called Annie, the tall blonde was Nicole. Nicole was elegant and graceful, and Annie was clumsy and always making fun of herself, grinning every time she fell over things or dropped something. Both girls nodded to André and he to them, but they didn't have much to say to each other. André was unusually quiet, and after a while he murmured something about going back into the water.

'Coming, Simone?' he asked, a glint of hope in his eyes.

Simone said no, not yet. She saw André's face crease in a frown, and knew he was hurt. It irritated her. She didn't belong to him. She was enjoying talking to Annie and Nicole. Although they were French, they were like Angie and her other girlfriends back in England. They were dressed like them, in jeans and shorts and T-shirts. Not like André and his funny black trousers and eccentric white shirts, and not like Grand-mère with her wooden clogs and black stockings.

Before long the three girls were chatting like old friends, discussing a film they had all seen recently.

'You must come to the cinema with us, in St-Jean,' Nicole said, naming the small town a few miles from Kerlennec. She smiled graciously, like a queen offering favours, but the words were friendly and sincere. 'Of course it will be in French, but you understand so well!'

Simone said that she would like that, and Annie grinned and hugged her impulsively, knocking over Nicole's coke as she did so. Nicole shrugged her shoulders resignedly, as if she was used to this, and gave Annie a playful smack on the knuckles before going off to find a cloth.

Then the girls said that they would have to go. Annie's mother was picking them up shortly. But first they walked back together to the rug, where Simone's mum was watching them expectantly. André was nowhere around.

Simone introduced them to her mum, and she could tell they were impressed at Mum's fluent French. Then Annie's mother turned up, and was introduced. Annie's mother was not at all like Grand-mère either. She was more like Mum, young-looking and relaxed, in a casual cotton skirt and a sun-top.

When the girls and Annie's mother had left, Simone lay on the blanket next to Mum. Out of the corner of her eye she could see André, still paddling in the lake – or sulking, as she suspected; even from the rug she could see that he was scowling.

'Are you getting used to Brittany now?' Mum said.

'Oh yes,' Simone answered. 'It's good to know there are some normal kids and grown-ups here.'

Mum propped herself up on the blanket and looked seriously at Simone. 'Your grandmother, and Monsieur Arragon, and even André, are all part of a life that is vanishing. Maybe that's good, or maybe it's bad. Whatever, it was your father's life, even though he left it to study, then to teach. All the young people go, in the end. There are no jobs, no opportunities for them here now.'

Simone, lying on her back, stared at the needles of the pine tree above her. Behind it the sky was a deep blue. The branches of the tree looked like tapestry, like the old ones she had seen in stately homes back in England.

'What about André?' she said lazily. 'Do you think he'll ever go?'

Mum was silent for a few minutes. 'Poor André,' she said at last. 'He seems to be caught between past and future.'

As if hearing his name, André reappeared, flapping his arms and shaking his long hair like Cassis after the rain. Now that the girls were gone, he had recovered his high spirits, whooping enthusiastically as he jumped up and down to dry off.

'Come on, Simone, let's play ball,' he shrieked, grabbing the two plastic raquets and foam ball that Mum had bought for them in Pontivy.

'*D'accord*,' Simone replied. 'I'm coming.' André dragged her to her feet and pushed her towards the open grass area. He was tugging and hanging on to her as if afraid she would suddenly vanish, and he would be alone again.

They had a good, energetic game. But Simone's mind wasn't really on it, and André went demented as he scored most of the points, yelling and hollering like a madman whenever she missed the ball. For once, it didn't annoy her. She was thinking of her two new friends, and the cinema she was going to in St-Jean with them this week-end. Mum had offered to drive them, and Nicole's mother would pick them up. At last, she was a real part of the village. She belonged here just as her father did.

Happiness filled her. She was even able to smile benevolently at that lunatic André, who was gloating in a most irritating manner just because he had won a stupid game. Well, let him, she thought. She had much more important things to celebrate.

Three

SIMONE BEGAN FEELING GUILTY ABOUT ANDRÉ A few days later.

It had to do with the film she and Nicole and Annie were going to see.

'It'll seem funny, dubbed in French,' Simone said as she was getting dressed to go out. She was in her bedroom combing her unruly hair into a green headband, which matched the new green T-shirt Mum had bought her in Pontivy.

'We'll have to leave soon. Is André ready?'

Simone put down her brush and looked at Mum. 'André?' She was puzzled.

'You did tell him about it, didn't you?'

Simone confessed that she hadn't even thought about it. 'It would be kind to include him, Simone,' Mum said quietly. 'He rarely gets a chance to mix with other children, and he'd love the film.'

'He goes to school, doesn't he?' Simone asked, annoyed at the thought of having André tag along. 'Where are all his school friends?'

'Grand-mère says he doesn't have any. He's an odd lad, as you noticed yourself, but you can understand why. He's isolated here at Truez-er Lann, with no one his age to talk to. And being half Spanish, he's always been something of an outsider, I suppose.'

'Like me,' Simone muttered.

Mum laughed, and put her arm around Simone. 'I think you're fitting in perfectly. I'm very proud of you, and so is Grand-mère.'

In the end there was no time to ask André, as it was late and Grand-mère had seen him in the back field, busy helping his grandfather feed the fat sow they kept in a small patch of ground.

'We'd better go without him,' Mum said, and Simone was secretly relieved. Though Nicole and Annie had been polite to André, she could tell they didn't really like him much.

It was a wonderful evening. The film was ace, and Simone met some other French girls, and boys too, her age. The boys weren't at all like André, she was glad to see. They spoke proper French, and wore ordinary jeans, and were like the English boys at her school back home.

Afterwards, they all piled into a crêperie and ate sweet pancakes filled with honey and lemon, melted chocolate and cream. Everyone clamoured around Simone, wanting to know about England. She was enjoying all the attention when an older boy who lived in St-Jean said, 'You're half French? What half?'

'My father,' Simone replied.

'He's done a good job, teaching you the language. You're pretty good.'

Simone flushed and was silent. The boy thought she was just shy or modest, but she didn't want to speak, didn't want to tell him that her father was dead, that it was her mother who had taught her French. She wanted to feel like she *did* have a father, who was alive and well and teaching her French. The boy would know the truth soon enough from the others, but for just a few moments she wanted to pretend.

After their crêpes they ambled into the town square, in front of the church, to wait for Nicole's mother. It was still light, though it was ten o'clock, because the clocks were an hour ahead in France.

'Well, what do you think of our friends?' Annie asked as she scrabbled around on the cobblestones picking up a bunch of centimes she had dropped out of her purse.

'You were a big hit with them,' Nicole smiled. 'I knew you would be.'

'They were sound,' Simone said. 'Not much different from my own friends at home.'

But how different from André, Simone thought. She wondered how many hamlets there were like Truez-er Lann which the young people had left, and felt a rush of pity for André. André had somehow got left behind and was trapped in a way of life that was dying out.

The little town of St-Jean was quiet, sleepy. A few old men hobbled across the square, nodding their heads, but that was the only sign of life except for themselves. Though Simone had thoroughly enjoyed the evening, she could see why young people in the small Brittany villages and towns left for the cities. There was not much for them to do all year round. Only the cinema – even the crêperie was shut in the winter evenings, according to her new friends.

That night, unable to sleep, Simone lay with the light of the full moon shining into her unshuttered bedroom. The moonlight gleamed on the roughly-carved wooden statue sitting on the shelf, the one of the old man with the beard, making it glow an unearthly silver colour. It was supposed to be of

Merlin, the Wizard, Grand-mère had told her, and Jean-Claude had carved it when he was thirteen or fourteen. He was good with his hands, Grand-mère said. At one time he had wanted to be a carpenter.

How Grand-mère must have missed her only son, Simone thought. How hard it must have been for her. A small twinge of sympathy went through her for the stern, forbidding woman who was her grandmother.

As Simone lay awake, kept from sleep by the moonlight but unable to bring herself to close the shutters, she thought she saw the wood-carving move. For a moment she was paralyzed with terror, until she realized that it was just a trick of the light – a cloud had passed over the moon. She chided herself for being so childish, like a kid seeing ghosts in every shadow.

In the morning, the room was bright with sunlight. Outside Cassis was barking playfully, and Simone could hear Monsieur Arragon talking to the dog in the old Breton language.

After breakfast Simone went to find André. He was scowling and bad-tempered.

'I saw you coming home last night, all dressed up like an American on the television,' he said as they were practising *boules* on Monsieur Arragon's dusty dirt track behind the house. Boules was a French game that Simone had learnt. The French seemed to play it everywhere, in the road, in special sand boule pits at the lake. It was a favourite of the old men, and Monsieur Arragon was an expert. André gave him a game often, and so, now, did Simone.

André threw his ball and knocked Simone's a good metre. 'So where were you last night?' André went on aggressively.

'Spying on me?' she asked angrily, but she felt guilty, too. André *would* have loved the film. And however odd and crazy he was, he was better than not having anyone at all at Truez-er Lann. She was even getting to like him, in a funny way. He drove her mad, he was childish and stupid sometimes, but he could also be clever and kind. When he wasn't clinging to her like a baby, he was surprisingly self-reliant, thinking up all sorts of interesting things for them to do.

'Yes, spying,' André said cheerfully. 'When your grand-mère said you had gone out, I waited in the apple tree till you got home. I saw Nicole's mother drop you off. You were with *them*.' He spat out the word scornfully.

'And what if I was?' Simone didn't look at André as she threw her last ball. 'I can go out if I want.'

André didn't know what to say. The truth of Simone's statement seemed to hit him like a stone. His face went pale, and his eyes grew even larger, more serious.

'I thought you were my friend,' he said plaintively.

He was so like a very small child, that Simone had to smile. She knew now that André was actually six months older than her, but sometimes he acted like a kid brother of five or six.

'People can have more than one friend,' she explained impatiently.

André thought this over carefully. His unruly hair fell into his eyes as he stared at his feet in deep concentration. 'Not me,' he said. 'One friend is enough for me.'

Then he took his last ball and threw it violently down the road. It hit a stone and bounced much farther from the tiny stationary goal than Simone's ball.

'I've won,' Simone said.

André didn't seem to care. He didn't say much for the rest of the morning, frowning and sulking until Simone, fed up, left him to join Mum and Grandmère shelling peas in the shaded courtyard.

Next day, Simone got out Grand-mère's old bicycle from the shed. The tyres were flat, but Mum drove to St-Jean and bought a pump and some bicycle oil. There was a huge straw basket on the front of the bike. 'You'll be able to go down to Kerlennec for our bread and milk,' she said smiling.

Simone took a ride that afternoon. A forlorn André stood at the edge of the road and watched her go.

'I can run and keep up with you,' he shouted as she pedalled away. His mood of yesterday had gone, and he desperately wanted to be with Simone.

'Don't be silly,' she shouted back. André stopped in his tracks. When Simone looked back she could see his hunched figure, as motionless as a statue, staring down the empty road. He looked as if he were being abandoned, as if this wasn't the only time he had stood at the edge of that road watching someone he loved go away.

Simone couldn't think about it for more than a moment or two. She was having trouble getting the hang of the old bike. There was just one gear, so getting up the hill was hard work. When Simone finally got to the village, she felt a real flush of accomplishment.

She bought bread at the *boulangerie*, milk and cheese at the local shop, then called in at a new bungalow on the edge of the village.

'Annie? It's me, Simone.'

Annie was out in a flash, her dark hair tumbling messily around her face and a faded denim shirt hanging half in and half out of her shorts. Her plump face beamed when she saw Simone. 'How did you get here? Did you walk?' she asked.

Simone showed her the bike. Annie laughed, but it was a nice laugh, and Simone joined her. 'I've never seen one so old,' Annie hooted. 'How brave of you to come all the way to the village on it. Wait until I tell Nicole!'

After a drink of fruit juice in the kitchen, Annie got out her own smart bike and they pedalled to Nicole's house. Annie was a terrible cyclist; she kept turning around to look at Simone and not looking where she was going.

'Look, Simone has wheels!' she shouted when they spotted Nicole sitting under a pear tree in her garden, reading a book and looking cool and poised in white shorts and a gauzy top. Simone felt sweaty and dishevelled, and suddenly shy and embarrassed all over again about Grand-mère's ancient bike. But though Nicole smiled when she saw it, she said it was priceless and asked if she could have a go on it.

It was a relaxing, easy afternoon. The three girls cycled around the village and ended up back at Nicole's house, playing with her three new kittens. Simone had brought her photographs of home, and Nicole and Annie exclaimed over them and said how much they'd love to come to England.

'You'll have to visit me,' Simone said. 'There's only Mum and me, and we have a spare bedroom with two beds. You can meet Angie, and we can go swimming at the leisure centre, take a trip out to Dartmoor . . .' The three girls talked on and on.

When Simone came home, André was sitting on the

road, right where he had waved good-bye to her hours earlier.

'You are so weird!' Simone cried, exasperated. 'You can't just sit waiting for me every time I go out for an afternoon.'

André hung his head. 'Will you come and play ball with me and Cassis?' he asked humbly.

'I'm tired, André. Maybe later.'

Simone went into the house. Grand-mère was teaching Mum how to make a Breton gâteau. They were both up to their elbows in flour and were laughing like kids.

After a while, Simone wandered outside again. She was feeling guilty about André and furious with him for making her feel that way. She didn't like the way he was so possessive about her, not wanting her to go anywhere, see anyone, without him. But she could understand how he felt. She remembered when she was five and had just started school in Exeter; she had clung to Angie, and Angie to Simone, like André was clinging to her now.

But we're older, Simon thought with exasperation. I learnt how to fit in. Why can't he?

Maybe some peole never do, she mused dispiritedly. André, with his funny face like a little wizard, his skinny short body, his quirky way of speaking, perhaps never would. But it wasn't surprising that he was an oddity – how could he be anything else? Never going anywhere, hardly ever seeing his parents, only an old grandfather to talk to . . . it made Simone feel creepy.

She played boules for ages that evening, in the long twilight, with André and Monsieur Arragon. She did it to start with because she felt guilty, but ended up, as she always did, having a good time. Monsieur Arragon played the game seriously, but with humour. He teased André gently when the boy got too boisterous and wacky, but Simone could tell it was with love. André was very fond of his grandparent. Simone wished she could feel that way about hers.

They had been in France for almost two weeks, and. Simone felt she hardly knew her grandmother. She avoided the old woman whenever she could, leaving Mum to chat to her, to help her with all the little chores around the house. There wasn't much to do anyway, other than tidy her room and help with the washing up. Her grandmother sometimes tried to talk to her about her life in England, but Simone always wriggled away and went out to find André, or to cycle to Kerlennec. She remembered to be polite, but she couldn't be responsive.

And then, when they had been there exactly a fortnight, Mum dropped her bombshell.

'I phoned Billy last night,' she said to Simone as they sat in the front garden, under the willow tree, eating crusty bread for breakfast.

Grand-mère didn't have a phone. When Mum wanted to ring Billy in England, she went to Kerlennec in the evening. Simone sometimes went too, when she wasn't outside playing ball with Cassis, or sitting in the apple tree with André, making up stories about King Arthur and his court. André had read the stories too, which surprised and delighted Simone. The two spent many happy hours comparing the stories they had read, discussing their favourite characters.

Simone loved the tales André made up about the Camelot heroes and villains. He told the stories brilliantly, especially the scary ones with characters like Morgan le Fay, the evil sorceress, and Mordred, the knight who tried to overthrow Arthur. There was one André told that made Simone's hair stand on end, full of witchcraft and stealth and evil spirits.

André acted out his stories too, telling the parts in different voices, waving his arms about a lot and making faces. Sometimes he gave Simone a role, telling her what to say and involving her in it so much that soon she was acting out the characters as well. That was one of the compelling things about André, the way he got her to do daft things like that. Somehow with André it didn't seem silly. He made her feel that they were actors, or story-tellers, or writers. He made them feel as if it were the most sophisticated thing in the world, to be sitting in an apple tree making up stories.

André's stories were something else. He had a lively imagination, and believed passionately in his own make-believe. He loved the Camelot myths, the tales of mystery and adventure, and many were set right in Brittany.

'This is a magic part of France, Simone,' André would often tell her. 'Brittany is full of ancient legends, and ancient spells and curses and enchantments. We had the Druids, and all those standing stones still dotted around, many more than your Stonehenge. The old spirits still haunt the place, you know. You can feel it all around you.'

'Aren't you afraid, then, with all those ghosts?' Simone chided kindly, humouring him.

'Oh no, because the enchantment isn't evil, not usually,' André answered seriously. 'Merlin the magician spent a lot of time in Brittany, you know, and he was a good wizard. He keeps the wicked spirits in line.' André was thoughtful for a moment. 'When he can,' he added quietly.

Simone wasn't sure if André was kidding her or not,

so she didn't say anything. And indeed, she could feel the magic. Especially at night, when she looked out of her bedroom window at eleven o'clock and it was still not quite dark. Night mists swirled around the gnarled willow tree, bats swooped in the moonlight – she could believe wholeheartedly then that Brittany was enchanted.

Simone, lost in her thoughts, suddenly realized that Mum had finished her breakfast and was talking to her about Billy. 'How is he?' Simone asked, wiping the jam off her lips with a tissue.

'He's fine.'

Mum and Simone were talking in English, because Grand-mère wasn't around. Mum had put down her bowl of coffee and looked at Simone. She was flushed and radiant, as if she were hiding a wonderful secret. 'We had a long talk,' Mum said. 'And I have something to tell you, Simone. Billy wants me to marry him.'

Simone's mouth opened in surprise. She was so shocked she didn't know what to say.

'I want to, Simone,' Mum carried on softly. 'Not since your father have I felt so happy with another man.'

Simone's thoughts were all in a jumble in her head. Of course she should have thought about this, but for some reason it never occurred to her. She somehow assumed that the relationship between them all would remain the same – Billy always being around, but that was all. Not moving in with them, not becoming one of the family.

Mum was watching Simone intently. 'I told Billy that I wanted to marry him, but that I wanted to talk to you first.'

'Me?' Simone stuttered. 'I'm not marrying him, *you*

are.' She attempted to laugh, but it sound strained and forced.

'I want to know how you feel about it,' Mum continued. 'I know you like Billy, but our home is your home too, of course. He would move in with us, when we're married. He's only in a tiny flat in the centre of town, and our house is big enough for the three of us.'

Mum looked at Simone expectantly. Her face was glowing like the little wood carving the other night, as if it were bathed in moonlight, or under some golden spell. Simone had never seen her look so happy.

Simone did the only thing she could do. 'That's great,' she exclaimed. 'Can I be a bridesmaid?'

As she said it, she knew it sounded false. But Mum didn't even notice. She was wrapped cozily in her own joy, hugging Simone, squeezing her hands. Simone went through the motions of responding, hating herself for not sharing Mum's euphoria. It was just the shock of it, she told herself, making her feel uneasy, apprehensive.

'What about Grand-mère?' Simone suddenly blurted. 'What will she think? Won't it upset her?'

'Your grandmother is a very wise woman,' Mum said. 'She knows about Billy and approves, but I'll wait until he comes here to tell her that we are getting married.'

Simone stared at Mum. 'Here? Billy? When?'

She was so distraught she was stammering. She hadn't had time to get used to the idea of Mum marrying Billy, and now he was coming here. She couldn't take it in. This was *her* territory, hers and her mother's. It was Jean-Claude's home. Billy had no right to come here.

Mum lay back in the deckchair, relaxed and satisfied now that Simone seemed to approve of her marriage to Billy. 'That's the other thing I have to tell you,' Mum said. 'I'm going off in a few days to meet Billy, down in the Pyrenian Mountains in the south of France. Billy knows someone who has lent us a one-room cottage there. I'm taking the train down, and Billy is taking his car through the Channel tunnel. He's in London now you see, doing a course. Then we'll drive back up here to spend the last few days of our holiday with you and Grand-mère.'

Somehow this was even more of a shock than the wedding announcement. 'But . . . but what about me?' Simone cried.

Mum, full of her wedding plans, her coming trip, was either unaware of Simone's distress, or unconcerned about it. She said, 'Now that you've made so many friends, I know you won't mind staying at Truez-er Lann with Grand-mère.'

Simone couldn't speak. The intoxicating scent of the roses coming from Grand-mère's garden suddenly made her feel sick. In the distance she could hear Cassis barking, hear the old sow snorting, hear André shout at her as he gave her her morning feed.

Mum was speaking again. 'It will be much better for you, staying here, than coming with Billy and me. It's even more isolated than this, the house in the Pyrenees.'

Simone still couldn't speak. Her stomach was churning and her thoughts were racing furiously.

'Besides,' Mum said coaxingly, 'your grandmother needs you. She'll be all alone again, after the summer.'

Simone looked with anguish at her mother. She knew that it was no good to argue, that everything had been decided. Without saying another word, she turned her back on Mum and ran up to her room.

She lay on her bed for a long time, with the shutters

closed. Mum and Billy wanted time alone, without her. She tried to tell herself it was understandable, that they wanted to celebrate their coming wedding. But it still hurt. Much as she liked Billy, she didn't want her mother to prefer his company to hers. But that was obviously what had happened. And that was obviously what would continue to happen, when they got married and Billy moved in with them.

They were getting married, Mum and Billy. The thought whirled around in Simone's head and she couldn't seem to get to grips with it. They were going away as well, the two of them, alone. Mum and Billy. They didn't want her around any more.

But Jean-Claude did. Simone looked miserably around the room, as if trying to find her father. *He* wouldn't have left her if he had lived. Shutting her eyes, she thought hard about him, evoking his image in her head. She began to feel his spirit surrounding her again, as if he were trying to tell her that *he* still cared, still wanted her. Oh, if only he were really and truly here!

All that was here was Grand-mère. Some stranger she didn't know, didn't want to know.

There were two, almost three weeks to get through, before Mum and Billy came back, and they all went home.

But what if Billy and Mum didn't come back? What if they stayed in the mountains, leaving her forever with Grand-mère? Simone knew that Mum would never do that, but she let her imagination run away with her. After all, she bet André never dreamt his mother would dump him in Brittany while she went off to work in Paris. Though André had said that his parents visited him when they could, they certainly hadn't been around since Simone arrived. They had obviously abandoned him, and if it happened to André, why shouldn't it happen to her?

Cassis was barking under her window, and André was there too, yelling at her to come down.

'Go away,' she cried, opening the shutters to shout at them both, then closing them again.

She wondered miserably if she was doomed to be a female version of André, dressed in long black wool skirts, living with a doddering grandparent, unloved, unwanted, becoming more peculiar by the minute, until no one, not even Angie, would have anything to do with her, ever again.

With the shutters closed, the bedroom was dark and shadowy despite the bright sunlight outside. The air inside was heavy, hot, oppressive. It felt as if it were seeping into her pores, contaminating her bloodstream. She felt as if she were being weighed down by mysterious forces, evil and malign. Her eyes fell upon the strange wood carving and in her depressed state she imagined that the stern figure of the wizard was mocking her.

Throwing herself on the bed and hiding her face in the soft feather pillow, she wondered whether she'd ever see England again.

Four

MUM LEFT TWO DAYS LATER. ANNIE'S MOTHER drove her to Lorient, to the train station, and Annie, Nicole, and Simone went too.

Simone let her mother kiss her good-bye, but didn't kiss her back because she knew she would feel like clinging to her like a baby if she did. Mixed with that, was a feeling of anger. Mum was dumping her with someone she hardly knew, in a forsaken place populated by misfits. And it was not as if she had any choice in the matter, like she had when she went off to visit her other grandmother in London.

When Mum had gone, Annie's mother took them all to a fancy crêperie where there were hundreds of crêpes to choose from, with all sorts of fillings, both savoury and sweet. Then they had a look around the city, going into shops, walking around the harbour area to look at the boats. Simone tried to perk up, she was still feeling low and miserable after seeing Mum go off, but she couldn't match Annie's bubbly mood or Nicole's quiet enthusiasm.

The light drizzle of the morning had vanished, leaving a clear hot sunny day. They drove a short distance from Lorient to a beach called *L'amour Plage*. They had brought swimming costumes and towels with them, just in case.

The beach was crowded, the water bracing but

refreshing. There were rows of cafés and shops lining the beach, and the three girls went for ice-cream after they had had their fill of sea and sun and sand. They sat at a white table under a yellow umbrella.

Although Simone had tried, nothing could lift her from her depression, not even her favourite ice cream. Trying to lighten up, she said, 'André introduced me to cassis ice-cream. Bliss.'

Annie, melted chocolate dribbling down her chin, rolled her eyes and exchanged a glance with Nicole, who was leaning back in her chair looking, as usual, graceful and assured. It's a good thing she's so nice, Simone thought, or she'd make everyone else feel gawky.

'André's peculiar,' Nicole said, licking her ice-cream.

'He's very bright in school in some ways, like writing essays and stories,' Annie interrupted. 'But then he's stupid in other things. He acts like a twit and shows off if you try to talk to him, or else he doesn't answer, and runs off like a scared rabbit.'

'So everyone just leaves him alone,' Nicole added.

Simone shrugged. 'He means well.' She knew everything Annie and Nicole said was true. What she couldn't explain was how sometimes André's showing off was endearing, like Cassis trying hard to please. Or how his stories, the ones he told in the apple tree, were magic, taking her far away to some other enchanted, fascinating world.

The day ended far too quickly. Soon Simone was home alone with Grand-mère, eating some kind of a stew she had made for them both. It was hot and

Simone wasn't hungry, but she tried to force some down to be polite.

She really missed Mum then. Simone used to let the two of them chatter away during meals, and didn't feel she had to say anything. Now, Grand-mère seemed to be expecting her to talk in the same friendly way as Mum. She just couldn't do it. She kept thinking of Mum and Billy, and how it would be back in England, the two of them wanting to be on their own all the time, without her hanging around. The more she thought about it, the harder it was to swallow. It was the longest meal she had eaten in her life.

Luckily André came in as Simone was finishing helping Grand-mère with the washing up. 'Come quick! Our sow has piglets!'

Simone ran out after André, with Grand-mère fast behind, stopping only to take off her apron and put on her wooden clogs.

Monsieur Arragon was leaning over the fence of the pig sty, looking fondly at the piglets. There were ten of them, all pink and tiny and squealing, trying to nudge in for a feed. The sow looked as if she didn't quite know what was happening.

After they had admired the piglets, Monsieur Arragon invited them all into his house for a drink to celebrate. Simone had been inside before. The kitchen doubled as a living room, like Grand-mère's. There was a wobbly table, a well-scrubbed stone floor, and two baggy armchairs by the wood fire, and that was all. But it didn't seem gloomy or depressing. Like Grand-mère's house, when the sun shone in the windows, it felt simple but clean and bright.

Grand-mère and Monsieur Arragon sat in the armchairs, drinking home-made cider. André and Simone were allowed a small glass, too. The cider was strong, and Simone felt a bit light-headed when they stood up to go home.

'Ah, the way the child turned her head!' Monsieur Arragon exclaimed to Grand-mère, as Simone shook his hand good-bye. 'It could have been Jean-Claude standing there.'

Grand-mère put her hand fondly on Simone's shoulder. 'She is Jean-Claude come home,' she nodded, 'but she also is not. She is herself, my beautiful grand-daughter. Something very special indeed.'

If Grand-mère had said that in front of Nicole or Annie, Simone would have died of embarrassment. But somehow in front of André, it seemed fine, and made Simone feel better than she had done all day. Her depression began to blow away like mist in a strong wind. How baffling that a remark of Grand-mère's could do that, when nothing else had.

They walked home in a peaceful silence. When Grand-mère put her arm through Simone's, she didn't mind it like she usually did when Grand-mère touched her. The old woman seemed less stern tonight, less formal. Perhaps it was Monsieur Arragon's presence, or the tall glass of cider she had drunk.

It was late, almost eleven, but it wasn't quite dark. Grand-mère lit the solitary lamp in the kitchen and sat back in the old worn sofa. She didn't seem to want to go to bed, nor did she tell Simone it was time to go up, like Mum did. She seemed relaxed, contented, and oddly enough, Simone did too.

Suddenly Grand-mère's face changed, and she bent double, as if she were in pain. No sound came from her, but her lined forehead creased up even more and her lips were pressed tightly together.

'Grand-mère, what is it?' Simone cried.

The old woman didn't speak for several seconds,

and just as Simone was about to run for Monseiur Arragon, Grand-mère managed a smile and slowly straightened up.

'It's all right, *ma chérie*,' Grand-mère said in a normal voice. 'Don't worry, my dear, I'm quite all right. A pain, probably indigestion. I'm fine now.'

She reached over to pat Simone's hand reassuringly. Simone, relieved, sat with her on the sofa for some time, and for once she did not find it awkward talking to Grand-mère. She even found herself telling Grand-mère about Angie. She did it to take both their minds off Grand-mère's pain, but once they got to talking, she found she was enjoying herself, and Grand-mère was listening with genuine interest.

Later, as she climbed the wooden staircase to her room, Simone glanced back at Grand-mère, who was watching her with a haunted look on her face – part joy, and part sorrow.

'*Bonne nuit, petite-fille.*'

'*Bonne nuit, Grand-mère.*'

Somehow, tonight, for the very first time, the words felt true. Tonight Grand-mère was beginning to feel like family.

Next day, sitting with André and Cassis in the garden, Simone was unusually quiet. André was rolling the ball to the dog who kept bringing it back and leaping playfully on both of them. Finally André said, shyly. 'So your mama has left?'

'Yes, but she'll be back,' Simone replied, more heartily than she felt.

André nodded gravely. 'Like my mama,' he said.

Simone looked at him, surprised. She nearly said, It's not at all like your mama!

Grand-mère had told her not long ago that André's parents had virtually abandoned him. 'I haven't seen

— 51 —

either one of them for many months,' she had said to Simone. 'It breaks his grandfather's heart, the way those two ignore their child. André waits and waits for his mother to come to Truez-cr Lann, and take him to Paris with her as she once promised, but she never comes. Poor boy.'

André met Simone's gaze bravely, as if he were daring her to contradict him. She didn't have the heart to say that his mother was never coming for him. Anyway, she was sure that, deep down inside, André knew this too.

So she just said, gently, 'Yes, like your mum, André.'

André hooted, his mood, as usual, changing abruptly. 'So in the meantime, we don't need anyone; we have each other, yes?'

He broke off as Cassis knocked him over, thinking André's excitement was the beginning of another game.

'Just you and me, André and Simone!' André shrieked as he and Cassis tumbled boisterously in the grass. 'André and Simone – and Cassis too – against the world!'

'What about the grandparents?' Simone laughed. 'Don't leave them out.'

André stopped playing with the dog and sat up, his mood changing dramatically once again. 'They're very very old, Simone,' he said sadly. 'They're not enough.'

He lay back thoughtfully on the grass, his eyes closed, pretending to be asleep. Simone prodded him to get up, but he wouldn't budge. She gave up and lay on the grass herself, staring up at cloud formations. It was ages before André came out of whatever sombre mood he was in and began larking about as if nothing was wrong.

The next few days were not as bad as Simone had expected. She missed Mum, and still felt hurt at being left behind. The anger hadn't gone either, so she tried to shut Mum out and not think of her. She would have been totally wretched if she hadn't been getting used to Grand-mère, feeling more comfortable with her.

Since the night in Monsieur Arragon's house, when they all drank cider together, Grand-mère had seemed more at ease with Simone, more talkative and forthcoming. She didn't watch Simone with that anxious look on her face, and she actually giggled, like a girl, when reminiscing about Monseiur Arragon as a young man. She seemed altogether more natural, softer.

Simone mentioned this to André, one day in the apple tree. André was chewing on a small, green crab apple which wasn't even near ripe.

'Of course your grandma feels more comfortable with you alone,' André said, munching away and ignoring Simone's warning that he'd get stomach-ache. 'She was nervous of your mother.'

'What?' Simone looked at him as if he were out of his mind. How could anyone be afraid of Mum – kind, easy-going Mum?

'Wouldn't you be nervous, if a long lost daughter-in-law from another country came suddenly into your life? I heard my grandpa and your grandma talking about it often, before you came here.'

Simone shook her head. 'That can't be true.'

André spat out a pip. 'Sometimes you are not very intelligent, Simone,' he said slowly, as if he were talking to a complete fool. 'Your grandmother is old and grew up quite poor, as did many of the old people working the land. She probably had to leave school when she was very young. She was afraid your pretty, clever mama would look down on her.'

'But . . .' Simone shook her head again. 'But I thought they got on so well!'

André looked smug, thinking he knew more about Simone's family than she did. He had his sombre adult expression on his face, which was such a contrast to the clownish monkey faces he pulled when he was excited or showing off. 'Of course they get on well. They have Jean-Claude to talk about, it brings them together. It's still easier for your grandma with you, for you're only a child.'

Simone resented André calling her a child, as if he were six years older than her rather than six months. But she had to admit it sounded logical.

'Hmm. Maybe you're right,' she shrugged.

André, delighted to be praised, and to show some superiority over Simone, plunged on. 'You're different too, with your grandma. Now that your mother has gone.'

'What?'

André nodded his head sagely. He was trying so hard to act the wise old man that Simone felt like throwing something at him. But she was curious as to what he would say. 'How am I different?' she asked.

'You've stopped trying to be so English.'

'But I *am* English, you idiot!'

André nodded again in his pompous, infuriating way. 'Of course,' he said importantly. 'But you're still half French. When your mother was here at Truez-er Lann, you talked to her, went to her when you needed

— 54 —

something. You didn't want to know your grand-mother. Now that your mama is gone, you have no choice.'

Simone shook her head, exasperated. 'I don't know what you're on about,' she said. 'You've been making up too many stories again, it's gone to your head.'

'Maybe you should use your imagination more, Simone,' André said. 'Then you'd be as clever as me.'

She *did* throw an apple at him then, and he pulled one from the nearest branch and threw it at her, and the whole apple tree would have been decimated if Grand-mère had not come out at that moment, laughing and saying, 'If you two don't stop, there will be no apples for cider-making in the autumn.'

Nicole and Annie cycled up to Truez-er Lann one afternoon. Simone hadn't been expecting them. She was in the middle of an intricate game with André, something he had made up with Jean-Claude's old Dominoes set and involving so many daft but imagi-native rules that they made Simone's head spin.

They were playing in the garden, sprawled out in the grass under the shade of the apple tree. Grand-mère was hovering around plucking the dead heads off her geraniums. She had on her outdoor clogs, her long black skirt, and a tattered kerchief on her head to keep the sun off. A strand of white hair fell over her eyes. When she saw Nicole and Annie, she gave them her lopsided smile and her crooked tooth gleamed in the sunlight.

Simone cringed. She was sure that the two girls would giggle at Grand-mère. They were too well-mannered to do it to her face, but Simone knew that as soon as Grand-mère turned her back, they would snigger, roll their eyes, make a face. She knew Angie would, back home. Not that she would mean to be unkind. It would just be a wordless acknowledgement that here was someone a bit weird.

But to Simone's surprise, Nicole and Annie both smiled genuinely at Grand-mère, and said hello warmly. Of course they knew her; they had grown up seeing Grand-mère, and Grand-père when he was alive, going into the village for provisions. They would be used to Grand-mère's strangeness, of perhaps she wasn't strange to them at all. Perhaps most people in Brittany had an old grandparent, or a great aunt or uncle, who was very like Grand-mère, or Monsieur Arragon.

It was a new thought to Simone. But she didn't have time to dwell on it long, because André was being a pain again, trying to attract the visitors' attention by talking too much, waving his long arms about and telling some loud but boring story about Cassis. Simone still couldn't get used to the way André changed from minute to minute, like a chameleon changing the colour of its skin. Yesterday André was giving her insights into her grandmother that were really quite sensible; today he was blabbing like a four-year-old.

This time Nicole and Annie *did* make a face, but it was about André, not Grand-mère. Simone saw them exchange looks as André went on and on, bragging about something or other. The more they looked bored, the more animated André became, as if he could force them to listen by becoming more and more frantic.

Simone wanted to sink into the ground. The two French girls would think that she was as barmy as André, hanging around him all the time. Simone liked her new friends, and suddenly felt panicky that they would get fed up, jump on their bikes, and ride away, never to return.

It was Grand-mère who saved the day. 'How hot it is!' she exclaimed, interrupting André in full flow. 'You must all be thirsty, especially you, Annie, Nicole, after your cycle ride from the village. Come into the kitchen where it's cool. There is sparkling mineral water, and blackcurrant cordial, and I baked some galettes this morning.'

As she talked she politely but firmly ushered them to the house, leaving André in mid-sentence. He looked rather surprised, but couldn't say anything because Grand-mère was old and you had to make allowances. Only Simone realized that Grand-mère wasn't absent-mindedly interrupting but had done it deliberately.

André tagged along to the kitchen, and Grand-mère made him a drink too. After they had eaten most of the delicious Breton biscuits, André started pulling the girls outside. 'You haven't seen my piglets,' he cried. 'My beautiful piglets!'

'I didn't know piglets were beautiful, André,' Nicole teased.

'Mine are,' he replied seriously.

So they all trooped out to the field to see the pigs, leaving Grand-mère making a fresh batch of galettes. André showed off the litter proudly, as if he had given birth to them himself.

'You must see Cassis now,' he ordered imperiously.

Annie and Nicole exchanged glances again. They had good-naturedly gone to see the sow and piglets, and had even enjoyed watching them for a while, but they had cycled all this way up to see Simone.

Cassis, who had been in the house with Monsieur Arragon, was called outside. 'Simone and I have a wonderful game with Cassis,' André said importantly. 'We throw the ball to her and she tries to hide it. You can play if you like.' He said it as if he were a king granting a wish to one of his subjects.

'It's too hot,' Simone protested, seeing how Nicole and Annie hesitated.

'Far too hot to run around,' Annie agreed eagerly.

'Why don't we go up to your room, Simone?' Nicole said pointedly. 'We can listen to music. I brought that tape you wanted to hear.'

'Great,' Simone answered, relieved. 'See you tomorrow, André.'

André had been about to follow them to the house but he stopped short at Simone's words.

'Thanks for showing us your piglets,' Annie said politely.

'Yes, thanks,' Nicole echoed, waving languidly as she followed Annie.

Simone led the way across the cobbled road to Grand-mère's house. She didn't dare look back at André, who had not uttered another word, but silently watched the three girls walk away.

That evening, after Simone had helped Grand-mère wash up their dinner plates, she felt restless. When Annie and Nicole had left, she had helped Grand-mère prepare crêpes for their evening meal, thinking what fun it would be to impress Angie and her friends back home with Breton delicacies.

Home. England seemed so far away. Simone had had a letter from Mum, a letter that made her think of bubbles in a foam bath, the way Mum's words burbled on the paper, full of light and colour and frothy delight. Everything was fantastic, Mum wrote. The

Pyrenees, the weather, their snug house. Billy was fantastic too, it seemed. Of course they missed Simone, but Mum was sure she'd be having a lovely time with all her new friends in Brittany . . .

Simone was low after she got the letter. Mum was clearly quite happy without her. She certainly didn't need Simone around, that was obvious. Would it be like this back in England, she wondered? Mum wouldn't need her at all when she and Billy were married. And they were going to be married in the autumn! Mum had sprung that on Simone in the letter, no date had been mentioned before. Secretly Simone had hoped that the wedding wouldn't be for ages and ages. That way she didn't have to think about it too much, for despite her reassurances to Mum, she still resented it. But Mum had written that there was no point in having a long engagement, and they might even get married in early October. It was August now.

Simone was thinking about the letter that evening. She had had one from Angie as well, but she kept thinking about Mum's, about Billy and Mum getting married so soon. Simone realized that until this letter she had not let herself truly believe it. But it was real, she had to face it. Where did that leave her? Mum and Billy had each other, she was the outsider. The thought so upset her that she couldn't sit still, and began prowling around the room.

Grand-mère was sitting in the massive armchair in the kitchen, having her usual after-dinner doze. Simone found herself wishing that there was a television in the house. Monsieur Arragon had one, and sometimes Simone watched over there with André. But she didn't want to go there tonight. She had told André firmly that she would see him the next day. She was somewhat surprised that he hadn't come around, after the girls had left. She half expected him and Cassis to come bouncing over after dinner, now that the evening was pleasantly cool after the hot day. Just right for a game of boules or a romp with Cassis.

But there was no sign of André.

Next morning he was still unusually absent. Simone didn't have time to look for him, as she was going to the beach with Annie's family. Nicole couldn't go because she had relatives arriving from Paris for a short visit, so it was just Annie, her mum, her little sister and Simone. Simone felt guilty about André. She had left him yesterday to spend time with Nicole and Annie, and today she was leaving him again. He'd be surly for days. Simone sighed, wondering why life was so complicated.

She was looking forward to this outing. She needed something to take her mind off Mum's letter, which was still eating at her like Cassis chewing the ball, unwilling to let go. Mum's eager plans for herself and Billy whirled around like flying demons in Simone's head, until she thought she would scream. Thank goodness she was going to the seaside with Annie's family, however bad-tempered it would make André.

The beach was near a town called Carnac, about an hour's drive away. They swam for ages in the cool green sea and then explored the sand dunes. Annie's mum had made delicious ham and cheese sandwiches in freshly-baked baguettes which they ate hungrily. When they had finished, they helped Annie's sister build a huge sand château. ' "A castle", we say in English,' Simone said, and smiled as the French girls tried to pronounce the word.

Annie's mum took them to Carnac, to see the tall

prehistoric granite stones, or megaliths, lined up in fields. The stones seemed to go for miles and miles. No one was really sure who had put them there, or why, but it had all happened thousands of years ago. André had said that it was probably the Druids, who were supposed to have built Stonehenge in England, but no one knew for sure.

There was a fence preventing people from going up to the stones and touching them, and Annie, grumbling that she'd like to get closer, tore her shirt poking around a broken bit of fence. Her mum sighed with exasperation, but said she knew another spot not far away where there were other megaliths, though not so many as in Carnac. They took the car and drove a few miles until they came to a dense pine forest, the tall trees looming majestically above them.

It was almost evening when they got there, still light and warm. A small sliver of a moon was coming up, yellow and mysterious against the impressive pine trees. Simone had never seen such massive trees before, and thought they looked eerie and powerful, as if they were the oldest things on earth.

As they walked, Annie's mother explained that there were different kinds of megaliths. Some might have been the altars for pagan ceremonies, years before the birth of Christ, or they could have something to do with the position of the stars. Many people felt that they had magical power, but the truth was, nobody knew much about them at all.

The megaliths that they were approaching were called *dolmens*. Dolmens were ancient burial chambers, thousands of years old. These stones were not the tall standing ones, but more like barrows or low caverns on the ground. There were about fifteen of the enormous stones, some placed horizontally on top of others, rather like a giant's granite table, to make a kind of chamber underneath where they buried their dead.

No one was at the burial site but them. There were no railings or fences to keep them away, so they climbed on top of one of the dolmen and then crouched in the burial chamber.

'Funny to think of all those people buried here, thousands of years ago,' Annie said as she and Simone crept around in the dry dirt under the massive stone. 'I wonder if it's haunted?'

They were silent for a moment. Annie's mother and sister were wandering around the edge of the site, and Simone noticed that a mist had come up, snaking in and out of the towering pine trees and gathering in the clearing where the stones were situated.

'André says all Brittany is haunted,' she murmured, but Annie didn't hear because she had already left the chamber to follow her mother and sister down the dirt track back to the car.

Simone lingered for a moment or two. The mist that had suddenly come down was chilly, damp, and it must have been *that*, that suddenly made her shiver: that or the vivid memory of one of André's more grisly stories about black magic and sorcerers. They were the only things she could come up with to explain the trembling that went through her body. An odd terror seized her, and she wanted to run like mad out of the burial chamber, down the track to the car, but her limbs felt heavy and paralyzed, as if the mist itself had turned malignant and was sapping her will.

Annie, her mum and her sister, seemed hundreds of miles away, though Simone could hear them laughing and chattering. In despair she tried to break the spell that was trapping her, but she couldn't move.

A shout from Annie set her free. 'Simone, where are you? Hurry up, it's getting late.'

Simone shook herself and wrenched away from whatever invisible bonds were holding her. Shaking with relief, she ran after Annie and soon caught up with the family. Seeing how normal they looked, listening to their laughter, Simone felt feeble-minded for her vivid imaginings in the dolmen and decided that she was getting as bad as André, believing in all that magic stuff.

But she had to admit that Brittany *was* extraordinary, with its old people in clogs, its ancient standing stones, its changeable stone houses which seemed grey and gloomy one minute, then happy and sunny the next. She thought about the ghost-like mists that came swirling out of nowhere, about the many mystical legends entrenched in the area.

This was where her father came from. *Her father*. She no longer mostly thought of him as Jean-Claude, she realized, but almost always now as her father. This was his country, and in some ways he was still as mysterious and unknown to her as the enigmatic people who had built the megaliths. Staying in the house where her father was born, reading his books, touching the things he touched as a child, and played with, and loved, she knew she was beginning to find him, but there was still something elusive about him which she felt he wanted her to understand.

As Simone walked away from the standing stones, she looked back one more time to see the mist thickening over them. In the quiet of the pine woods, a bird screeched suddenly overhead, frightening her with its intensity. She thought the bird had shrieked out her name before it flew off beating its heavy wings.

'Are you all right?' Annie asked. 'You look funny.'

Simone shook her head. 'That bird. Didn't it sound . . .' She broke off. It was too crazy to tell Annie.

'It sounded peculiar, didn't it?' Annie agreed. 'I've never heard a bird quite like that.'

Simone was glad when they reached the car, and glad too that everyone was tired after their long day out and that nobody felt like talking. Annie's mum switched on the car radio, and above the music Simone kept thinking she heard that spooky black bird, calling her name. Suddenly she missed Mum, and though she was with people she liked, she felt terribly, unbearably, lonely.

She would have liked to talk to André, but when Annie's mum finally brought her home, it was late and she was tired. André was nowhere around, and of course Grand-mère wanted to hear all about her day. When Simone finally got to bed, she was asleep in an instant. In her dreams she saw her father, looking troubled and sad for some reason which she didn't understand. He called her name, and his voice sounded like the strange bird she had seen soaring above the megaliths. Then his voice faded and it was gentle but faraway, calling to her, telling her how happy he was that she had come home at last. When she woke up the first thought she had was that even if Mum didn't want her anymore, her dad did.

Five

AFTER DOING THE BREAKFAST DISHES AND SWEEP-
ing the stone floor for Grand-mère, Simone went
outside to look for André. She was surprised that he
hadn't appeared after breakfast. He usually did,
rushing in the kitchen with Cassis at his heels, full of
plans for the day.

It was going to be another scorching day. The bees
around the honeysuckle were madly busy, their
buzzing noise sounding like a distant tractor. A few
hens had got out from the chicken run behind one of
the barns and were scratching in the garden. Simone
shooed them away from Grand-mère's young plants
and walked across the road to find André.

Monsieur Arragon was in his garden, investigating
his roses. He told Simone that André was cleaning out
the sow's pen. She thanked him and went out to the
back of the house.

'*Bonjour*, André,' Simone called.

André looked up at her, then looked down. 'Oh,
bonjour,' he said coolly, carrying on working as if she
wasn't there.

'Do you want a hand?' Simone asked.

'No. I'm almost finished.'

André worked in silence until he finished mucking
out the pen. Then he said, '*Au revoir*,' and started to
walk away.

Simone, frustrated, called after him. 'Do you want a game of boules, before it gets too hot?'

'No, thank you,' André said politely but without even looking back at her. Then he was gone.

Simone walked reluctantly into the house. André was brooding, of course, as she suspected he would be. He was cross with her because she had been out all day yesterday without him. If Mum had been here, she'd have said that it was rude not to have invited André to the beach, but it wasn't Simone's fault that he hadn't been included. It was Annie's mother who had invited *her*, and she couldn't very well ask to bring a friend along. Especially a boy that Annie didn't like very much.

The morning dragged slowly. Simone hadn't realized how much she relied on André's company. She helped Grand-mère with some hand washing, wringing the wet clothes out and hanging them on the clothes line in the courtyard. Grand-mère didn't have a washing machine, and every week she washed the sheets and towels and all their clothes by hand, though Mum of course helped her, as did Simone. Mum had suggested taking them to the launderette in Pontivy, but Grand-mère wouldn't hear of it. In many ways life had hardly changed in Brittany for the last fifty years, Simone thought as she struggled with a wet sheet.

Cassis wandered over, and Simone took her for a romp in the field behind the house. There was still no sign of André.

Nicole was tied up with her relatives from Paris, and Annie was off to a dentist's appointment, or else Simone would have cycled in to Kerlennec. Instead, she went inside and began a letter to Mum, but stopped because the letter sounded glum and miserable. Not that Mum would care, she sniffed, feeling

sorry for herself. She was having too much fun with
Billy. Simone abandoned the letter and wrote to Angie
instead.

It seemed to be the longest morning since Simone
had arrived in France. The afternoon was getting set
to be the same, when Monsieur Arragon casually
knocked on the kitchen door and was asked inside.
'I'm taking André to the lake for a swim,' he said to
Simone after greeting Grand-mère. 'Would you like to
come?'

Simone agreed enthusiastically, not stopping to
think that this was out of the ordinary, because
Monsieur Arragon rarely drove his old brown Citröen
any farther than the village and back, and occasionally
to St-Jean to the market on Thursday. She grabbed
her towel and swimming costume and said good-bye
to Grand-mère.

In the antiquated Citröen, which Monsieur Arragon drove at about 20 miles an hour, André said
glumly, 'I didn't know Grand-père was going to ask
you to come along.'

Simone decided to ignore him, until he stopped
acting like a spoiled, sullen child. Luckily, the minute
they got to the lake, his mood changed and he became
his noisy chattering self again.

Simone was relieved. André could be good fun, and
she didn't want another long morning like today. On
the other hand, she wasn't about to give up her
Kerlennec friends just because he got in a mood
whenever she spent time with them.

It was too gorgeous a day to be worried about that
right now. A welcome breeze cooled the scorching air,
making it just right for renting a paddle boat and going
out on the lake. Monsieur Arragon had said he wanted
to treat them to the boat. He gave them a few francs

and then went off happily to the boules pitch near the café where he was soon involved in a game with some other elderly Frenchman.

André made so much noise on the boat that he scared away two swans that were swimming nearby. After paddling furiously for ten minutes or so, he and Simone sat back and drifted around the middle of the lake, watching some ducks playing about on the water.

Simone was lying back, eyes closed, when she heard André say, curtly, 'Oh, it's you.' When she opened them she was surprised and pleased to see Nicole paddling up in another boat next to them. With her was a stocky boy a year or so younger.

'This is my cousin, Philippe,' Nicole said. 'From Paris.'

Simone said hello and André just grunted rudely. 'We'd better be getting back,' he said to Simone, ignoring the other two.

Simone glared at him. 'Don't be silly, André. We have plenty of time before we have to bring the boat back.'

'Let's have a race!' Nicole shouted. She and Philippe started pedalling vigorously towards the other side of the lake.

'Good idea,' André said grimly.

'Easy, André,' Simone said as André kept poking her to pedal faster. 'This is supposed to be a game, a bit of a laugh.'

'I want to win,' André shouted. 'Come on, get going. Why are you so slow?'

André's face was red with fury and strain as they tried without success to catch up with the other boat. 'If we win,' he said, 'then you have to be my friend for the rest of the summer. If Nicole wins, then you can be with her.'

Simone almost stopped pedalling, she was so astounded. 'You are so ridiculous!' she shouted. 'That is so childish. How many times do I have to tell you that I can have as many friends as I want?'

André didn't answer. He was pedalling so furiously that Simone's legs were whirling, trying to keep up with him. Soon they had pulled past Nicole and Philippe and were well ahead of them.

'We won!' André shrieked. 'We won, we won, we won!' He stood up and began jumping up and down.

'Stop that!' Simone yelled. 'You'll tip the boat over!'

As she said it, André leapt again with excitement, and tripped over into the water.

The lake was deep, the shore still distant. 'He can't swim!' Simone shouted. She knew her swimming wasn't strong enough to jump in and rescue André, so she leant over and tried to grab him as he bobbed up. But he was too far away. Just as he was going under again Nicole jumped in after him, and before either Simone or Philippe could move, she had pulled him up and was swimming with him towards the boats.

Somehow, Philippe and Simone managed to pull André into the boat, with Nicole holding him and helping to push him up. André was shaken, but quite all right. Slowly, they made their way back to the sandy side of the lake.

'Don't tell Grand-père what happened,' André pleaded with the others.

Nicole looked at him severely. 'You are a very stupid boy,' she said sternly, as if he were years younger than her and not more or less the same age. 'I won't tell your grandpa if you will promise not to do such a barmy thing again.'

'I promise,' André said meekly.

Nicole stared at him. Though she looked as

unruffled as ever after her plunge in the lake – her yellow hair wet but sleekly plastered to her face, her swimsuit already beginning to dry in the hot sun – her voice shook and Simone noticed that her face, despite its light tan, was deathly pale.

'You could have drowned,' Nicole went on. 'And you nearly tipped Simone into the water too. You must learn to swim. We have swimming classes at school, but you're always too busy messing around to pay attention and learn. So now you'd better.'

'I will, Nicole,' André said, chastened.

The four of them, after they had brought back the boats, lay sprawled on the hot sand, exhausted and shaky. André was silent and subdued for the rest of the afternoon, even when Nicole and Philippe had said good-bye and gone back to their family picnic on the forest side of the lake.

'Are you all right?' Simone asked.

'Yes.' André wouldn't look at her, but buried his head in his arms and pretended to be asleep.

That evening André and Simone sat in the apple tree. André had bounced back somewhat since his mishap, but he still wasn't his usual boisterous self. 'Come on, how about one of your stories?' Simone said encouragingly. André's preoccupation was making her uncomfortable.

André, unusually, was reluctant, but Simone egged him on until he finally got started. But it wasn't like his usual stories, which were full of fantasy and adventure and excitement. Tonight's story was about a lost boy, who had to find his way home by a difficult journey, and in the end never got there.

It was a gripping story, as André's tales always were.

But Simone knew it was different, though she couldn't think exactly how.

It wasn't until she was drifting off to sleep that night that it came to her. André's story was *real*, something that could almost happen to him or to her or to anyone their age. It wasn't full of magic and wizards and imaginary heroes and villains. André's story was all about people like themselves.

Simone wasn't sure whether she liked this or not. Trying to decide, she fell asleep.

Next day was stormy. Great black clouds gathered from all directions and a high wind rattled Simone's shutters as she got out of bed.

By the time breakfast was over, it was pouring with rain. André burst into the kitchen looking like a great mud puddle himself, in rubber boots and a grimy brown waterproof. His long hair was dripping with water and his face looked as if he'd just come out of the lake.

'I've been sitting in the apple tree,' he exclaimed, jumping on one foot around the room. He had recovered his high spirits after his escapade the day before.

'In this storm? You're crazy,' Simone said.

'I was watching the lightning sizzling in the distance. And listening to the thunder. It sounded like a hundred wizards casting spells. Don't you feel it, Simone? Don't you feel the thunder enchanting you?'

As he said this he began to prance around the kitchen mischievously, caught in his own make-believe. A sudden peal of thunder made him cackle with laughter as Simone jumped.

Grand-mère began to scold, as she would a young

child. Simone thought how often people had to speak to André as if he were a little boy. 'Take off your wet coat, and your boots,' she ordered. 'You're dripping water everywhere. Warm yourself by the fire.' She fussed over him like a baby, giving him a towel to dry his hair and offering him a galette.

André took one of the butter biscuits and crunched on it loudly. A peal of thunder broke overhead and when it finally stopped, André said, 'Come on, Simone, let's go up in the apple tree and watch the lightning.'

'You will not,' Grand-mère said. 'The storm is right above us. It's far too dangerous.'

André pouted. 'What can we do, then?' he whinged.

Grand-mère looked at him thoughtfully, then at Simone. 'Would you like to go up in the attic?' she asked. 'There are some things there of Jean-Claude's that you might find interesting.'

Simone had never been up in the attic of the old house. She and André climbed the outside steps and pushed open the heavy wooden door. A frightened swallow flew out of a tiny hole in the side.

'The swallows always build their nest here, in that corner,' André said. 'Every year I've watched them flying in and out.'

The attic was warm and dry, despite the torrential rain outside. Pitted beams propped up the roof and the floor was made of wooden slats, dusty and splintered with age. One small window, floor height, looked out over the front garden, the willow tree, André's house.

At first the attic seemed empty in the shadowy light. 'There's nothing here,' Simone said with disappointment. She looked out of the window at the driving rain twisting the willow branches into ghostly shapes, but a cry from André made her turn around quickly.

André pointed to a large, old-fashioned trunk in the corner of the attic. It was unlocked, and Simone and André began to take out her father's old belongings. There were some metal toys, trucks and cars and tractors. There was a pen-knife, the blade dull and rusty. There were his exercise books from school, carefully written out in his neat French handwriting.

André began racing around the attic with one of the toy trucks, running it around the floor and making lorry noises at the top of his voice. 'Oh, what fun!' he said excitedly, entranced by the toys. Simone remembered that André had very few possessions, and smiled as she watched him play with these new-found treasures. Sometimes Simone felt she lived a life of great richness and luxury, compared to André's life in this stark place.

Turning away from him, Simone sat down on the wooden floor and began reading a small notebook. It was some sort of diary, written in a childish hand by a young boy. The diary was full of ordinary things like going to school, or playing in the village, but on the last page there was an enthusiastic entry about going to some forest called Brociliande, where Merlin and the other characters of the Camelot tales were supposed to have lived.

'I've never heard about this Brociliande,' Simone said, showing André the passage. 'King Arthur's people were supposed to have lived in the West Country of England, either in Tintagel or Glastonbury or somewhere.'

'Trust you English to take all the credit,' André said scornfully. 'Everyone in France knows that Sir Lancelot and Guinevere and lots of others came to Brittany some time or another. Lots of the Camelot stories take place here.'

Simone was intrigued, but also a bit upset. She had never known that. All these years she had been reading about Camelot, day-dreaming about her father doing the same thing, yet in reality he had been engrossed in a completely different version based in France. It made her feel uneasy, as if she hadn't known him at all, the way she thought she did.

She didn't want to think about it. 'I wonder what else is in this trunk?' She began rummaging around, André right beside her.

Outside the rain was still lashing down, and the thunder still rumbled with a deep ominous noise, like a troll gurgling. The storm seemed to be hovering around the house, circling it, as if it intended to stay forever.

'Look at this,' André exclaimed. He began to pull out some old posters and laid them on the floor. Simone looked, fascinated. She recognized, even without reading the French writing, that they were all of Camelot. One was very like the one on her bedroom wall in England, of the Round Table itself, with all the Knights, splendid in their armour. There was one of Sir Lancelot, under a weeping willow tree, standing next to Queen Guinevere, and even a dark, rather frightening poster of the evil knight Mordred, who had plotted to overthrow King Arthur. Mordred was standing with his wicked mother, the enchantress Morgan le Fay, and they both looked so malign that Simone quickly went on to the next one.

'These are wonderful,' Simone exclaimed. The posters, though old, were in excellent shape, their colours faded slightly but still bold and vivid. Simone looked through them all, saying, 'Look how many there are of Merlin the magician. More than any of the others.'

'I know,' André replied. 'Jean-Claude must have been fond of Merlin, there are lots of books on him, too. That little wood carving in your bedroom, that your father made. That was supposed to be Merlin, you know.'

'Well, that's a relief,' Simone said laughingly, though Grand-mère had already told her. 'At least Merlin was a good wizard, not an evil sorcerer.'

'Magic is magic, Simone,' André said mysteriously. 'Don't ever underestimate it. Especially not in Brittany.'

Simone shivered, thinking about the other day when she had imagined she was being imprisoned in the dolmen. She thought about the megaliths in Carnac and in the pine forest, the burial chambers which refused to give up their secrets, the cries of mysterious birds, the wood carvings that seemed sometimes to glow with life, the silvery moonlight coming through her window at night. 'I would never underestimate Brittany's magic,' she said fervently.

'Did you see these?' André's voice broke into her reverie. 'Look, all the photos of your father, when he was a boy.'

Simone had seen photos in the house, of course. Grand-mère had several in frames, of Jean-Claude as a child. But those were formal photographs, like school photographs. The ones André was handing her now were snapshots, in black and white, of a boy playing with a cat, sitting in the apple tree, grinning and waving at something or someone behind the camera.

His hair was thick and unruly, and he had a wide mouth, with slightly protruding teeth. Simone felt eerie, as if she were looking at a ghost of herself. Everyone had said how Simone looked like her dead father, but she had never seen it as clearly as she was seeing it now.

'Creepy, isn't it,' André commented, looking from the photos to Simone, and back again. 'Are you sure you're not a ghost?'

Simone shook her head and shuddered. It *did* feel creepy; it gave her goosebumps. The growling of thunder still rumbling over the house didn't help either.

Suddenly, Simone didn't want to be in her father's house, or even in his country, much as she was getting to know and love Grand-mère, much as she was beginning to enjoy the part of her that was half French. There was something uncanny, unearthly, that seemed to her to be gathering around the house, around *her*, just as the storm was still ominously hovering overhead.

'Come on, I'll race you,' she shrieked to André, determined to thrust these morbid thoughts from her head. Like a demented five-year-old, she grabbed a tractor and went 'Brrrooom, brrrooom,' across the attic floor, making André yelp with delight as they raced around, almost drowning out the noise of the storm outside.

That evening the storm still raged. It was more like late autumn than midsummer, with the leaves blowing off the trees from the sheer force of the wind.

André wanted Simone to go over to his place to watch television, but Simone said she'd stay home with Grand-mère. The lights were flickering in the storm, and Simone was worried that the electricity would be cut off, leaving Grand-mère in the dark. Simone found herself wondering what Grand-mère did on her own all winter, when the relentless cold and wet kept her indoors, without her rose garden and her geraniums to potter about with.

Grand-mère was sitting at the kitchen table, reading the local newspaper that Monsieur Arragon had brought up from the village that morning. Simone, curled on the huge sagging sofa, was reading a book, in English this time. It was one she had brought over with her. The storm was abating slightly, the rain not as heavy, the wind dropped. The lights still flickered now and again but the power stayed on.

After a while Grand-mère looked up from her newspaper and smiled at Simone. 'Jean-Claude was a great reader, like you are,' she said. 'Grand-père was always telling him he'd ruin his eyes, reading all hours of the night when he should have been asleep.'

'What did he like to read?' Simone asked, putting down her own book.

'Ah, everything. Fairy tales when he was younger, then adventure stories full of heroes and good deeds. And then as you know, he became passionate about the King Arthur stories. Do you know that many were set in Brittany?'

'André was telling me that today.'

'There were several Bretons at the Round Table, you know,' Grand-mère went on. 'Jean-Claude told me all the stories. The knight, Sir Tristan, was Breton, and there were others too. And some people say Sir Lancelot was French.'

'He wasn't!'

'His father was thought to live in Vannes, on the coast not too far from here. He and King Arthur were good friends, and Arthur visited him often.'

Simone was silent. She had never known any of this: her books and the films she had seen had set all the stories firmly in England. Once again she felt uneasy, as if her father were suddenly drifting away from her, or as if she had never been as close to him as she had imagined.

'There is a forest called Brociliande, in the old stories,' Grand-mère went on. 'It is not far from here, maybe an hour and a half drive away. The legends say that Merlin met the sorceress Vivian there, and fell in love with her. Later *she* enchanted *him*, using his own magic. Some say that Merlin is still there, entombed forever under the spell. There are many mythical stories attached to Brociliande.'

'My father went there, I know,' Simone said. 'I read about it in an old diary of his.'

Grand-mère stared into the distance, past Simone, past the kitchen table, as if she were looking at something very far away. 'Jean-Claude was fascinated by Brociliande,' she said dreamily. 'Grand-père and I took him there when he was about your age; no, younger, I think.'

'I know. He wrote all about it in the notebook.'

Simone and Grand-mère were silent for a moment. Grand-mère was in some world of her own, and Simone noticed how much less stern she looked in the flickering light. She didn't look like a witch at all, she thought, in spite of her snake-like coil of hair, her crooked tooth. She looked like . . . well, like someone's grandmother. Like *her* grandmother.

Grand-mère began to talk again. 'It is not just in reading that you are like Jean-Claude,' she said. 'He used to play with Monsieur Arragon's daughter, the one that works in Paris now. André's mother. Like you and André, they used to climb that apple tree, swim in the lake.'

'Was André's mum as weird as he is?' Simone asked.

Grand-mère waited until a distant growl of thunder had passed. Then she said, 'She was not so excitable, no. But perhaps to you and your English friend, she *would* seem strange, just like Jean-Claude would. They were both country children, growing up on isolated farms that had not changed in a hundred years.'

'I suppose I'd seem strange to *them*,' Simone mused. 'Me and my friends.'

'Everyone seems strange, until you get to know them. Isn't that true, *ma petite*?' Grand-mère smiled kindly at her.

Simone thought about how she felt about Grand-mère at first, how her feelings had changed. 'Yes, it's true,' she admitted, smiling back.

Grand-mère went to the cupboard, reaching for a tin on the top shelf. 'It's time for our galettes, and a hot cup of chocolate,' she said.

But as she said this she suddenly gasped, and fell back against the table. With both hands she tried to prop herself upright although her hands were trembling like the leaves of the apple tree in the high wind.

'Grand-mère, what's wrong, is it the pain again?' Simone said, but by the time she had got to her grandmother, the old woman had steadied herself. 'It is nothing, *petite enfant*. Absolutely nothing. See, it is going now.'

Simone helped her to the sofa. Grand-mère looked pale but she was composed. 'Do not look so distressed, Simone,' she said. 'I am old. Old people have many aches and pains. It is quite normal.'

'Should I call Monsieur Arragon?' Simone asked worriedly. 'He can go for the doctor.'

'*Non, non, non,*' Grand-mère exclaimed with a little laugh. 'He has enough aches and pains of his own. I wouldn't think of troubling him with one of mine.'

Grand-mère was looking a bit better now, but Simone was still concerned. She insisted on making their nightly chocolate drink, and Grand-mère was happy to let her do it. They drank it together, in an easy silence, and by the time they had finished, Grand-mère seemed fairly normal, though Simone wondered if she were still in a bit of pain as she was very pale.

Simone stayed awake a long time, thinking of Grand-mère. She's so old, Simone thought. She wondered how Grand-mère would get on in the winter, her first one without Grand-père. She had Monsieur Arragon opposite, of course, but he was just as old as Grand-mère, and besides, it wasn't the same as having someone in the house. Perhaps Simone could ask Mum to have a telephone installed. At least that would be something.

That is, Simone thought hazily as she was drifting off to sleep – that is, if Mum cared anymore about Grand-mère. She had Billy: she didn't need either Simone or Grand-mère. A dreadful melancholy seeped into her, making her toss and turn restlessly.

Before her eyes finally closed in a deep sleep, Simone was sure she saw Jean-Claude standing by the shuttered window, the dull rain making a monotonous sound behind him. Jean-Claude looked sad, as if he knew Mum no longer cared for him either. She had replaced him with some Englishman, just as she had replaced Simone.

Simone wanted to call to him, to tell him that she'd never forget him, never stop loving him. She was ashamed of her traitorous feelings in the attic that afternoon, when she too had wanted to run away from Jean-Claude.

'I won't leave you, like Mum is doing now,' she muttered fitfully, not knowing if she were asleep or awake.

But she knew somehow that Jean-Claude had heard her promise and was pleased with her.

Six

ANOTHER LETTER CAME FROM MUM. THIS TIME
Billy wrote too, adding a few lines to the end of
Mum's. He said that they both missed Simone, but
that she wouldn't have had much to do in the
mountain village where they were staying. He wrote
that Mum talked so much about Simone, she might as
well be there!

Well, why did she leave me behind, if she misses me
so much? Simone thought. She flushed with anger as
she read the letter again. She felt as if she had been
tossed aside like a torn book, a broken toy.

The anger evaporated as quickly as it had come,
leaving her drained and desolate. She looked up to see
Grand-mère watching her. 'So?' Grand-mère asked.
'Your mama and her friend are enjoying their holiday?'

Simone shrugged. 'They seem to be,' she said
grudgingly. 'Mum goes on and on about the beautiful
views from the cottage, about the long walks they take
around the mountains.'

Grand-mère looked at her shrewdly. 'You don't
mind being left behind, to stay with your old grandmother, whom you hardly know?'

Because this was exactly how Simone *did* feel, when
Mum first left, she felt herself blushing and stammering incoherently. She was disconcerted by Grand-

mère's words, how acute they were.

But before Simone was forced to answer, Grand-mère laughed and said, 'But we have not done so badly, eh, *petite-enfant*? You and I? We have managed all right, just the two of us.'

Relieved, Simone found herself going to Grand-mère, spontaneously giving her a hug. 'We've done fine,' she beamed. 'Just fine.'

Simone went upstairs to stuff Mum's letter out of sight in the drawer of her dresser; she certainly wasn't going to answer it yet. Her anger at Mum returned as she banged the drawer shut. When she looked up she cried out with shock – Jean-Claude was there, right in front of her!

But on second glance, she saw only her own reflection in the dresser mirror. Uneasily, she glanced around the room at all the familiar objects, for reassurance, and her eyes fell on the wood-carving of Merlin. The statue stared out at the room as inscrutably as always, and everything else was also exactly the same.

Still, she wouldn't look into her mirror again, though she told herself she was just seeing things. Hastily, she ran back down the stairs.

The day they went to the forest of Brociliande, the storms cleared and summer came back to Brittany.

The four of them set off early one morning: Monsieur Arragon, Grand-mère, André and Simone. Simone didn't think the dilapidated Citröen would make it – the forest was almost 80 kilometres away – but Monsieur Arragon assured her that the car, though old, was sound and reliable.

Grand-mère and Monsieur Arragon were jittery

with anticipation, more so even than the children. Monsieur Arragon had had such a good time at the lake the other day, that he had persuaded Grand-mère to leave Truez-er Lann and go back with him a day or so later, one afternoon between storms. Grand-mère had enjoyed the lake. She had watched André and Simone swim, and Monsieur Arragon play boules. She had even smiled and joked with the other boules players, some of whom looked even older than she was.

The visit was such a success that it was Grand-mère who had suggested the outing to the forest of Broci-liande. She remembered how Jean-Claude had loved it, and she wanted Simone to see it too. Monsieur Arragon was game. His two trips to the lake had exhilarated him, and he was ready to coax the old Citröen into going farther.

They made a good early start, for André's grandfa-ther refused to drive on anything but back roads so the journey was bound to take a long time. They went through lovely deep valleys, and past fields and fields of sweetcorn growing tall and green. The roads they took were usually empty. There seemed to be so little traffic in Brittany, Simone thought. She mentioned this to André, who only said, 'There have always been more spirits than people in Brittany.'

They stopped on their way in a town called Josselin, where there was a towering château by a magnificent river. It looked like a castle right out of a fairy tale, with its grand round turrets and its high stone walls rising like a cliff above the river. Monsieur Arragon took them for a *café au lait*, and Grand-mère was grinning and blushing like a young girl; it was the first major outing she had had in years.

They sat at an outside table overlooking the castle.

Grand-mère kept gazing wide-eyed at everything: the German and Japanese tourists with their huge cameras, the English at the nearby table trying to order tea with milk. Simone couldn't help noticing how the tourists stared at her grandmother. But then she was wearing her best long black dress with velvet sleeves and white lacy apron, which stood out starkly amongst all the pastel shorts and T-shirts. On her head was the lace *coiffe* that Grand-mère had worn the first day Simone arrived.

At first, seeing people staring at her grandmother, Simone felt the old embarrassment again. But then she realized that those who stared were doing so with interest, even delight, for here was a genuine Breton woman and not just another tourist. No one was sniggering or laughing. Simone even saw an English-woman in a lurid pink shellsuit trying to sneak a photograph of Grand-mère when she wasn't looking.

'Look at that wonderful old woman!' the English-man with her exclaimed, not realizing that Simone could understand. 'How dignified she looks.'

'I managed to get a snapshot of her,' the woman replied.

Simone smiled to herself, wondering how embarrassed *they* would feel if she suddenly started speaking English.

The forest of Brociliande was cool and mysterious. They stopped first at Le Val-sans-Retour where the wicked enchantress Morgan le Fay had lived.

'She still does; can't you feel her lurking around?' André said as they walked up a dirt track towards the valley.

Both Grand-mère and Monsieur Arragon were

puffing by the time they reached the barren plateau that overlooked the valley. They decided to sit right there and not go a step further. Some clouds had come up, light foamy ones, bringing a welcome breeze and some shade from the sweltering sun.

André and Simone ran down the rocky path, through the oak trees, and down to the lake at the bottom of the valley. There were no people around, only some hikers way off in the distant hills. The breeze had grown stronger, making a moaning sound in the full leafy branches of the many oak trees.

'You can see why they call it the Valley of No Return, can't you?' Simone said, looking at the sharp craggy rocks at the side of the lake. 'It feels creepy down here.'

'You can almost hear Morgan le Fay calling her victims,' André agreed.

'Who were they?' Simone wanted to know.

'Oh, the Knights of the Round Table. She used to lure them to this valley and cast a spell on them.'

'Did they die?'

'I suppose some of them did. They probably still do.'

'Don't be daft, André. There are no Knights of the Round Table around now.'

'You're so sure of everything, aren't you, Simone,' André exclaimed placidly. 'It never occurs to you that there might be things that cannot be explained, things of another world that we know nothing of. Maybe you're in for a shock one day.'

Simone wanted to mock André but instead she shivered at his words, even though the sun had come out again and the secluded valley was stifling hot. She thought about seeing Jean-Claude's reflection in her mirror. She had not once looked into that mirror since, because she knew with an ominous dread that instead of her own eyes, she would see the sad, haunted eyes of her father. She told herself it was only because of the photographs she had seen in the attic, that looked so like her, but she still took her hairbrush downstairs to brush her hair in the bathroom mirror, and avoided her reflection in the bedroom.

She never told André these things. He was so highly strung, and believed so strongly in the spirits of Brittany, that he'd only make it worse somehow, frightening her even more. And she *was* getting frightened. No matter how she tried to convince herself it was just her own imagination, combined with André's tales of magic and enchantment, she felt in her heart that there was something more, something she herself didn't want to face.

The Valley of No Return was so still that Simone thought she could hear a leaf rustle in a beech tree high above her. And then, suddenly, a piercing shriek stabbed the hot air and a great black bird went soaring over the tree-tops.

'Did you hear that?' Simone gasped. 'What was it?'

'A bird, I suppose,' André retorted. 'I didn't see it.'

'It was black and looked huge. And it had an awful cry.'

André shrugged. 'It's just this valley, full of echoes. It must have been a crow or something.'

Simone wasn't convinced. 'Let's go back,' she said. 'I've had enough of this place.' She knew she was being wimpy but the bird had unsettled her.

As Simone followed André up the rugged track leading out of the valley, she felt as if something were tugging at her T-shirt, pulling her back, back, back, into the Valley.

'André!' Simone shouted, terrified. But as André

turned around the mysterious force ceased, and Simone couldn't swear that it was not just a sudden breeze that had pulled at her.

'What is it?' André called.

'Nothing,' Simone muttered. Thank goodness they were near the top, she thought. There was something about Le Val-sans-Retour that made her tense, jumpy.

'Jean-Claude, your father, was fascinated by this valley,' Grand-mère said to Simone as the four of them took one last look before turning to go. 'Grand-père and I could hardly get him away.'

Simone was trembling again, as she had that day in the pine forest, when she lingered behind in the stone burial chamber. Perhaps that was how her father had felt in the Valley of No Return, that same inexplicable paralysis that Simone had felt at the dolmen, as if something was keeping her there against her will.

Jean-Claude was dead, but perhaps his spirit was trapped, tied to the valley, to Brittany, to Truez-er Lann. Maybe he was waiting to be freed. Was that why he kept appearing to Simone, out of the corner of her eye, in the mirror, in the shadows of trees, in that misty space between dreaming and waking? Did he want *her* to free him? Would he keep haunting her until she did?

Simone shook her head hard, to get these fanciful ideas out of them, and told herself she was letting this spooky place get to her.

They went next to Merlin's Tomb, which was a mysterious circle of stones covered in flowers and wreaths of twigs and branches that people had put there. It was deep in the heart of the woods, but luckily there was a dirt track not far away where Monsieur Arragon could take the car. The old people would never have been able to walk as far as the tomb in the heat.

'I'm sure Merlin's still here, like the old stories say,' André said with a hush in his voice. 'Vivian, the sorceress, imprisoned him, but he wanders around to this day, trapped in Brociliande.'

A tremor went through Simone. André's eyes were gleaming with awe, but hers looked frightened. The wizard's tomb was dark, smothered in dense shadows from the trees around it. 'You can't tell me there's no magic here,' André whispered as he and Simone stood staring at the stone circle.

Simone silently agreed. She was glad when Grand-mère announced she was hungry and ready for lunch. Simone was feeling quivery again, and hoped that food would calm her.

'Come, let's find a picnic spot,' Monsieur Arragon said. They followed him through the woods, carrying baskets of food and drink.

'This is perfect,' Grand-mère said, stopping at a grassy clearing between the trees. The forest was shadowy, ancient, filled with old oak and ash and beech trees.

Grand-mère had packed thick crusty Brie sandwiches, with tomatoes as fat and tasty as the freshest fruit. They ate peaches and nectarines, and drank sparkling water from a battered cooler which Monsieur Arragon had produced. The old man had also carried two creaky folding chairs from the car, which he set up under the trees so that he and Grand-mère could sit comfortably.

André and Simone lazed on a tartan rug on the

grass. When lunch was finished, the grandparents closed their eyes and had a little snooze. André and Simone lay on their backs on the blanket and watched the cloud shadows weaving in and out of the trees.

'Come on, let's have a look around,' André said, unable to sit still for long. He got to his feet and began tugging at Simone to get up.

Simone was restless, too. It was so quiet at this time of day; even the birds had stopped singing, and the breeze that had rattled the trees earlier had died down. It was very hot. Deeper into the forest it looked cooler, inviting, but Simone hesitated, not wanting to venture further.

'Come on, Simone,' André nagged. 'It's stifling here. There's more shade further on. Besides, I want to explore.'

Reluctantly, Simone followed André into the woods. He was unusually silent as they walked along, mesmerized by the stillness. The forest seemed petrified, unreal. Sunlight fell in patterns under the gnarled trees, making dazzling whirls of brightness in between the shade. The ground was soft and springy with moss and wild grass. Now and again they stumbled on great pine cones, almost as large as the ones Simone had found with Annie by the megaliths. There were a few creaky pines scattered between the oak trees, but not many. André started to collect the cones, but they were so big that he left them in a pile under a young ash tree.

'In memory of Simone and André, who were here,' he said grandly, bowing theatrically to the cluster of cones.

Simone shivered. 'Don't say that. In memory of means you're dead.'

André shrugged. 'Well, when we're dead, the pine

cones will be our tombstone. Merlin's got one here, so we can be part of the legend of the forest, too.'

Simone shivered again. It had suddenly grown dark in the forest. The bright patches of beguiling sunlight had gone, leaving only gloomy shadows.

'We'd better go back,' Simone said. 'We've been gone ages.' She was uneasy and troubled. The stillness of the forest had gone. Simone thought she could feel it moving, rustling, quivering with something sinister and frightening.

'Yes, we'd better turn back,' André agreed. He too was uneasy about the forest now, plunged suddenly into such unexpected gloom. 'Perhaps a storm is coming up; it's got quite dark.'

They walked back much more quickly than they had started out. But after a while, when they should have been approaching Grand-mère and Grand-père, André said, 'This doesn't look familiar. Look at that uprooted tree, those massive roots. I'd have noticed that if we passed this way before.'

They agreed that they must have taken a wrong turning, and retraced their steps. When they got to a dying beech tree with a hollow trunk, Simone said. 'We didn't pass this either.'

André and Simon looked at each other with dismay, admitting that they were lost.

'Don't worry,' André said, trying to be brave but feeling butterflies in the pit of his stomach. 'We can't be far away. And there's lots of daylight yet.'

Simone felt butterflies too. She knew that it wouldn't get pitch dark until quite late at this time of year, but because the sun was now obscured by thick clouds, it *felt* like night was fast approaching.

'We'd better start shouting,' André said. 'They'll hear us, and shout back.'

Simone agreed. 'They are probably just behind the trees, not far away,' she said hopefully. 'We just can't find them because the woods are so thick.'

They started hollering then. They called and called, and then stopped, and were very quiet, hoping to hear an answering shout from the two grandparents. But no one answered their cries. When the echoes from their own voices died down, there was nothing in the forest but a waiting stillness, intensely quiet and somehow threatening.

Except for my father, Simone thought suddenly. *Jean-Claude is here too, I can feel it.*

She didn't say it aloud to André, because he would think she had completely gone crazy. But as the long afternoon wore on, as they stumbled, in tears now, deeper and deeper into the forest, knowing they were utterly lost, Simone saw her father's face everywhere, in the thick foliage of the trees, the shadows of stones and copses, in her head when they finally, exhausted, sat down on the ground in despair. She felt that he was enticing her deeper and deeper into the magic forest, but why, she wasn't sure.

'Don't worry, they'll find us,' André said reassuringly, though he was just as frightened as Simone. 'I think we should stop wandering about now and just sit still. Grand-mère and Grand-père will go for help, and someone will find us soon.'

'I know, I know,' Simone said. 'I'm just so tired. And thirsty, too.'

'I'll tell you a story,' André said suddenly. 'About this forest. A nice story, I promise.'

Without waiting for her to say she wanted to hear another of his stories, he began a rambling tale about friendly talking animals who lived in the woods and helped lost children find their way home.

Simone had to smile, for although it was a simple story, more suitable for small children than for her and André, he told it with such imagination that he made her laugh, in spite of the tears threatening to well up again.

So she listened, even though she had long outgrown talking squirrels and hedgehogs. She listened because she knew André was frightened too, and was telling the story to cheer himself up as well as her. He was doing it also to keep the deep, silent forest at bay, to stop it from stealing over them both, casting a spell on them both . . .

When the story ended, it had got dark. Neither one of them could pretend that the day would last forever, not even this long summer day which had started out so bright and cheerful.

André fell quiet. He huddled closer to Simone, and they clung to each other, trying to keep their bodies from quaking in terror and from the chill that seeped into the woods when the sun went down. They were only wearing shorts – even André had abandoned his heavy black wool trousers and had bought himself some shorts at the market in St-Jean – and T-shirts, and it was getting quite cold. Simone had scratches on her face and hands from pushing through undergrowth, and André had a deep cut on his knee where he had fallen over a rotting log on to a sharp stone.

The forest was suddenly not so quiet any more. Simone could hear unfamiliar rustlings around her. She told herself it was only the harmless animals of the night, mice and rabbits and maybe even badgers, coming out to find food.

An owl hooted. Something black flew dangerously close to them before vanishing in the dark.

'A bat,' André said. 'It's all right. Bats are quite nice. We have them back home, around the farm.'

But Simone knew it wasn't a bat. Once again she could feel her father hovering around, trapped in the forest just as she and André were trapped. She wanted Mum, so much that she nearly cried out for her. But Mum was gone, miles away, not knowing nor caring where Simone was now.

As she closed her eyes so that she wouldn't see the grotesque shadows around her, Simone heard Jean-Claude calling to her. He wanted her to join him, wanted *her*, not like Mum who no longer did. She had go to him because he needed her, even if she too became nothing more than a ghost, a spirit.

Silent tears trickled down Simone's face. She would never get back to England now. Filled with despair, she promised her father that she would never reject him. She would stay with him always, whatever the cost.

Seven

*T*HEY WERE FOUND IN THE MIDDLE OF THE
forest just after midnight, by a search party from
the small town of Paimpont. Simone and André had
fallen asleep and were woken by the bright light of a
torch in their faces, and the excited cries of their
rescuers.

They were brought to Paimpont, to a stately Abbey
standing on the shores of a wide tranquil lake, where
Grand-mère and Monsieur Arragon had been given
shelter and food by the monks, though neither of them
could eat anything. The leader of the search party, a
stocky man called Gérard, had telephoned the Abbey
with his mobile phone to let everyone know the
children were found safe and sound.

Neither Grand-mère nor Monsieur Arragon could
even scold when they saw Simone and André. Both
cried, and so did the children, and the monks smiled
and made thick black coffee and sweet hot chocolate
drinks for everyone.

André's grandpa looked pale and exhausted, and he
kept shaking his head and clutching André as if he
couldn't quite believe the boy was real.

Grand-mère was holding on to Simone fiercely and
weeping big fat tears. She too looked white and
drained, and when she loosened her hold on Simone,
she clutched her chest.

'Grand-mère, what is it?' Simone cried.

'*Rien*. Nothing at all, my child, now that you are here, safe and well.'

But Simone noticed how her grandmother's face became even paler, and how her breath seemed to come in harsh, shallow gasps.

Monsieur Arragon noticed too. 'What is it, my dear?' he asked. 'Are you in pain?'

'It is nothing,' Grand-mère repeated, and managed to give them all a reassuring smile.

The monks brought them food: slices of cold meat, warm bread, a mixture of cheeses, lovely fresh pastries. The children ate hungrily, and even Grand-mère and Monsieur Arragon had something. Grand-mère seemed better, Simone was relieved to see, but she still felt worried about the old woman. She had been devastated by the children's disappearance, and Simone thought it was a wonder she hadn't had a heart attack or something, with all the worry and strain. She was getting on, after all. Simone would never forgive herself if anything happened to Grand-mère because of her.

'*Je suis désolé, Grand-mère,*' Simone whispered, after they had eaten and were resting in the huge lounge of the Abbey, all heavy wooden beams and old leather furniture. 'I didn't mean to frighten you.'

Grand-mère smiled, and to Simone, she looked beautiful. Her thick snake-coil of white hair had fallen down her back and wisps of hair were falling around her face, which looked even more wrinkled and crumpled than before.

'Don't be sorry, *ma chérie*,' Grand-mère said. 'You did not mean to get lost, and all ended safely.'

That night they slept at the Abbey. The monks had prepared two rooms, each with two narrow but comfortable beds. Monsieur Arragon and André shared one room, and Simone and Grand-mère the other.

Simone fell asleep at once. Her cuts and bruises still hurt, but the monks had cleansed them with medicinal herbs and oils and they were starting to feel soothed.

Her dreams weren't soothing, though. She dreamt that Jean-Claude was holding on to her arms, trying to keep her, and then from out of nowhere Mum and Billy were trying to pull her away, rescue her from his grasp. The worse part of it was, that in the dream she kept seeing her father's anguished face as Mum and Billy struggled to free her.

She woke up before either side could win.

Next day, after a breakfast of fresh bread and butter and black coffee that the monks prepared for them, the four visitors were asked to see a reporter from the local newspaper. Gérard, their rescuer, had told everyone in the town about the children and their escapade, and the locals wanted more details, and photographs.

The reporter talked to Simone and André, who told her all about their adventure in the forest. Then she chatted to Grand-mère and Monsieur Arragon, and got the photographer to take a photo of the old couple, as well as of the children. Grand-mère looked rested, though still pale, and her hair was neatly wound around her head again, her white *coiffe* perfectly in place. The reporter, a pleasant woman with red hair who said she was from Provence, talked to Grand-mère a lot. Grand-mère liked her, and told her all about Jean-Claude, and how Simone was his daughter, in Brittany for the first time.

André loved all the attention. He became cheeky

and talkative and silly again, until Simone had to give him a slight kick in the shins, which didn't have any effect. So she gave him the raised eyebrows, withering look, the one that Nicole used on him. André actually calmed down, and acted almost normal for the rest of the interview.

They finally began the two-hour journey home. Monsieur Arragon drove even more slowly than usual, as if making sure there would be no more mishaps. But everyone was in a good mood, and the trip went quickly.

Cassis was overjoyed to see them. She had been left in Monsieur Arragon's back garden, with plenty of food and water to see her through the long day. One of the neighbours had put out more water for her in the morning, when Monseiur Arragon did not return. He rushed over to explain where he had been, with André right on his heels so that he could once again tell of his adventure.

Grand-mère looked tired. She said, 'I think I will lie down for an hour, Simone, have a short sleep. We were in bed so late last night.'

Simone nodded. She still felt guilty at causing her grandmother such a fright. But Grand-mère patted her hand and said, 'I'm glad we went to the forest, *ma petite*, in spite of our mishap. Jean-Claude loved it there. He'd be happy to know you have been there too.'

He *did* know, Simone thought: he was there, he called to me, wanted me to come to him.

As soon as she thought this, she felt confused, disoriented. She went to her room. Her head felt fuzzy, as if it were no longer capable of grasping things.

Simone lay down on her bed. Jean-Claude's bed.

But where before, she had felt comforted and happy knowing that she was sleeping on her father's old bed, the one he had as a child, she now felt troubled. She could feel his presence all around her, once again trying to tell her something.

Perhaps he didn't want her to live with Billy!

The thought struck her suddenly, like a flash of lightning in a summer storm. Perhaps Jean-Claude was unhappy because Mum had turned her back on him, just as she had done to Simone. Mum was marrying again; she had found a replacement for her first husband. No wonder Jean-Claude was grieving. Perhaps he thought Simone would reject him also, let Billy replace him as her father. She'd never do that! Billy was Billy, not another dad. The thought had never even occurred to her, but maybe that was why Jean-Claude was lost and bewildered, unable to rest.

But could spirits be lonely and unhappy? Simone didn't know. She wished Mum were here so that she could ask her, but Mum had never seemed farther away.

Everyone in Kerlennec had heard about the adventure by that afternoon.

Simone and André were throwing the ball to Cassis in the back field when they were interrupted by Nicole and Annie shouting for them. The girls had come up on their bicycles, Annie nearly running over one of Grand-mère's geranium pots in her excitement and Nicole as cool-looking as if she had just stepped out of a shower, although she had just cycled up a long hill. They were both eager to hear the whole story.

'Were you scared?' Annie asked, when they had got to the part when night was coming and they knew they were hopelessly lost. Her round plump face looked frightened for them.

'No, not me,' André bragged.

Simone shot him a funny look but didn't say anything. Annie said, 'O la la,' in an admiring way, rather like Angie would have done at home only she would have said 'oh my' instead of 'O la la'. Simone hadn't though of Angie for a long time now, though they had exchanged quite a few letters.

Nicole lifted her cropped head and looked down her nose at André with a slight frown. 'You are even more dim-witted than I thought, not to be frightened. Alone in the forest at night, after hours of shouting for help and not knowing when, if ever, you'll be found – well, only a complete idiot would not be at least a tiny bit frightened.'

André looked startled, then sheepish, and then said, 'Well, I suppose I was just the teeniest, tiniest bit afraid.'

Nicole laughed and said, 'I should think so.' Then André started to laugh, and then Annie and Simone, and the four of them laughed so hard they had to lie back in the grass until they could get their breath back again.

'Should we play cards?' André said, when they had finally stopped giggling.

'If you can play sensibly,' Nicole warned him. 'If you start acting like a stupid little boy again, we'll leave you out.'

Once again, Simone was surprised at how meekly André accepted criticism from Nicole. Ever since the accident at the lake, when Nicole had rescued him, she treated him like a severe older sister, or even an aunt or a mother.

Maybe that's just what he needs, Simone thought as

they began the card game on the garden table, under the shade of a willow tree. Maybe he needs someone to mother him, because his own mother has left him.

Whatever it was, it worked. André acted like a normal boy his age, and the card game was great fun.

'They're not so bad, are they,' André exclaimed, as they stood and waved good-bye to the girls as they pedalled away towards home.

'I could have told you ages ago how nice they were,' Simone retorted.

André stuck out his lower lip in the familiar pout. 'They haven't been very nice to me. Not at school, and not here when you arrived.'

Simone made a face at him. 'Don't be so pathetic,' she said. 'Didn't it ever occur to you that it was *you* who wasn't very nice? You can put people off, you know.'

André made a face back at her, but he didn't argue or sulk anymore.

The day had turned showery, so they spent the rest of the afternoon in the attic looking through Jean-Claude's trunk again. Simone was drawn to the old photographs. She particularly liked the one of her father in the apple tree, sitting on the same sturdy branch where she sat with André. The tree looked gnarled and craggy even then, when Jean-Claude was a boy. Simone wondered how old it was, how many generations of children had sat in its branches.

André and Simone went through the posters once again. Their favourite one was of the forest of Brociliande with lovely coloured drawings of all the characters who were supposed to have lived there.

Since their experience in the forest, André had become even more obsessed with the Camelot stories and the legends that surrounded it. Though he had many books of his own, he found several more in Jean-Claude's collection and kept reading out bits to Simone, especially any concerning Brociliande. For once, Simone didn't want to hear them. Her own alarming adventure in the forest was still too vivid in her mind.

'Let's go downstairs,' she blurted, in the middle of a story André was reading. 'It's too dark up here.'

André insisted on taking the poster of the forest downstairs; he wanted to trace King Arthur's adventures in Brociliande.

'You must take that back to England, and anything else you want of your father's,' Grand-mère said. 'He would be very pleased.'

Simone didn't say anything. A few weeks ago, she would have been overjoyed to have something belonging to her father, when he was her age. But now, she just saw it as another hold Jean-Claude had on her, and she wasn't sure she wanted that. The trouble was, she wasn't sure of anything any more.

'Come on,' André said, tugging at the sleeve of her T-shirt. 'Let's spread this poster on the kitchen table. It's huge!'

It was a beautiful poster, despite its fading colours. On a broad outline of the map of Brittany, all the characters in the Arthurian legend were boldly and colourfully drawn, as were all the places which were prominent in the legends.

'Look, Simone, here's the Valley of No Return,' André shouted, forgetting himself again and pounding Simone so hard across the shoulders that she winced.

'Calm down,' Simone grumbled. 'I can see it.'

They found Merlin's Tomb on the map, and the town of Paimpont. André tried to figure out the exact spot where they had got lost, but Simone didn't want to know.

André jabbed his finger on the map and yelped. 'Look, this could be where we stopped for our picnic. It's near Merlin's Tomb—'

'Oh, stop, stop!' Simone's voice, loud and strident, rang in her own ears. André looked up from the map in surprise. Luckily Grand-mère had left the room.

'What's up?' André asked. 'What's wrong?'

'Nothing.' Simone was flustered. 'We've *been* to Brociliande, we've done that. Can we talk about something else for a change?'

She spoke harshly, and André frowned, hurt. Simone couldn't meet his eyes. She looked down and saw that she was still holding the photo of Jean-Claude which she had brought downstairs from the attic. That was how she'd like to remember her father, not like some haunted reflection in her mirror, or a spirit clutching at her.

André was peering at her nervously when she raised her eyes. 'Well, what shall we do, then?' he asked cautiously.

He was so jittery, terrified that Simone would walk out on him, that she felt ashamed. She wished he wasn't so vulnerable sometimes, like a scrawny, orphan kitten.

'Why don't you tell me a story?' she asked, trying to make amends. 'One of your realistic ones, though. *Definitely* nothing about witches or magic.'

'Don't you like those any more?' André was crest-fallen.

'I'm just not in the mood. But they're ace stories, honestly. You should write them down.'

André beamed, thrilled at the compliment. 'I hate to

write things down,' he said. 'I'd much rather tell stories.'

'Well, soon I'll be gone, you know, and who will you tell them to then?'

André looked so shocked that Simone said, 'You knew I was going back to England at the end of August. It won't be long now.'

André turned his back on her and pretended to look at the map. To her horror, Simone saw that he was crying.

'Oh André, what's the matter?'

He brushed his face with the back of his hand and sniffed a few times. Then he mumbled, so that Simone could hardly hear, 'Everyone leaves me, in the end. Everyone.'

Simone felt a sharp wrench inside her as she thought of André's mother and father, of all the young people who once lived at Truez-er Lann and left, of the children in the village who would grow up and go off, most never to come back. And poor André, left behind.

'I'll come back,' she said. 'Mum has long holidays, being a teacher, and we'll both come back to visit.'

'Everyone says that,' André sniffed. 'They never do.'

Simone knew that André was thinking of his mum and dad, and didn't know what to say. The two sat there silently for a few moments. Outside the rain had stopped, the sun was sliding out from behind the clouds. They could hear the murmur of voices, Grand-mère's and Monsieur Arragon's, wafting in from the front garden.

Simone suddenly remembered Billy, remembered that Mum would be too busy with him to want to go anywhere with her any more. 'I'll tell you what,' she said to André. 'I'll leave Mum behind, and visit on my own. I'm quite old enough. Mum could put me on the ferry, and maybe your grand-dad could meet me in Roscoff, now that he's getting into taking trips in his old car. It's not far.'

This cheered André immensely. Then he looked all droopy again. 'What's the matter now?' Simone asked.

'I'll have no one to tell my stories to when you're gone. I've never had a friend before,' he confessed.

'If you write them down you can send them to me. I'll read them all.'

'Will you? Promise?'

Simone promised. 'If you write them down, maybe Nicole and Annie will read them, too. If you behave and act sensibly,' she added, remembering how Nicole kept André in line.

This time André remained cheery. '*D'accord*, it's a deal! And now here's a new story, a nice one just for you.'

They settled down into the lumpy sofa and André began to speak. Though the story was intriguing, and not in the least bit scary, Simone couldn't concentrate. The memory of that day in Brociliande was still fresh in her mind. She had been badly frightened, and though she tried to tell herself that it was only a mishap, something that could happen to anyone, she still felt spooked when she thought of it. The more she thought of that afternoon, when she and André had got lost, the more she felt certain that she had somehow been led there against her will.

Had it been Jean-Claude? She couldn't help asking herself.

As soon as she thought this, she felt guilty and confused. Jean-Claude was her father. He loved her, or would have loved her had he been alive. But maybe he was angry, jealous of Billy, jealous of Mum and Billy getting married.

Simone shuddered. She had to stop thinking these things. But even now, the experience of the forest far behind her, she couldn't help feeling that something was not quite finished. Even here, in this gloriously sunny kitchen, she was filled with a nameless, indefinable dread, and knew somehow that soon she would come face to face with her father at last.

Eight

*F*OR THE NEXT FEW DAYS TORRENTIAL RAIN showers poured down, and then cleared as quickly as they had come. André dragged Simone up into the attic to play-act tales of magic and adventure when the storms raged, then, when the scorching sun came out, they sat in the apple tree.

Simone followed André as if in a dream. She had given up trying to drag him into the real world; she was just grateful to have him around. Nicole and Annie both were away somewhere with their parents, so Simone couldn't be bothered to cycle to Kerlennec. She felt too apathetic to bother about anything.

Simone preferred it when the sun shone and they were in the apple tree. Grand-mère had told her to keep the photo of Jean-Claude sitting in the tree, and Simone cherished it, feeling that this was the Jean-Claude she could be close to, the nice normal boy who, like her and André, loved the apple tree.

It was in the attic that the other Jean-Claude appeared, in the dusty beams, the pitted splintery wood floor, the many dark shadows. André told his stories and Simone could feel her father lurking about, listening, trying to get her attention, trying to tell her something she couldn't seem to grasp. Sometimes, when she felt him especially near and pressing around her, she wanted to grab André and run as fast as she could out of the attic, but she couldn't seem to do it. Her head ached, and her limbs felt heavy. She felt so lethargic that she could only lie on the hard floor, staring up at the cobwebbed beams, listening to André's tales.

André was so involved with his stories that he didn't notice Simone's lethargy. The magic forest had inspired him, and he was practically living in the fantasy world he had created for himself. Simone couldn't blame him. What else did he have, besides fantasy and legends?

One day the rain never stopped, and André and Simone stayed in the attic all day, even taking a picnic lunch up there, at André's suggestion. Simone meekly went along with it. She felt incredibly tired, and her head felt heavy, aching. She blamed it on the thundery weather.

André, digging into the trunk again, found some more photos of Jean-Claude hidden in an old rucksack that they had thought was empty. He was older in these photos, a young man. He must have looked like that when he died, Simone thought. She stared, mesmerized, at her father's face, his eyes. They were so mournful, haunting, piercing into her heart, sadly, accusingly.

That night Simone went to bed early, telling Grand-mère she thought she might be getting a cold. Grand-mère looked worried, but Simone convinced her that it was nothing, that she'd be fine in the morning.

It took her a long time to fall asleep; despite her fatigue, she was restless. When at last she dropped off, her dreams were troubled. First she saw Jean-Claude calling to her, then weeping as she ran away from him and into the arms of her mother and Billy.

At first she tried to pull away from them. They

didn't want her, didn't need her. But Mum turned her around to look into her face and Simone knew she had been wrong, knew Mum *did* want her, would always need her. Simone clung to them both, to Mum and Billy, and felt the heat of their love burning her like fire.

And then she saw Jean-Claude. His face was scarred with grief and torment. She was back in her own room – *his* room – and he was there, walking out of the mirror and beckoning to her.

The rain had cleared and the night was starry. A half moon glowed in the open window and seemed to light up her father's face like a beacon. Then he disappeared, and Simone knew that she must follow him.

Silently she padded down the stairs in her bare feet, her nightshirt gleaming white in the darkness. As she opened the door and went out of the house, Cassis barked in the distance, but Simone wasn't even aware of it. She was only aware of her father, leading her on, calling her to follow.

The grass in the garden was wet from the evening's rain as Simone walked across it. So was the apple tree, which she climbed easily, despite the dark. She had done it so often that summer, just as Jean-Claude had done it all the summers of his young life.

Simone looked out into the starry night and saw Jean-Claude silhouetted in the moonlight. 'Come, Simone,' he was saying. 'Come home to your father. I've been waiting for you.'

Simone reached out her hand but he was too far away. 'Come, Simone, come,' he whispered. 'Be brave, for my sake.' He held out his arms and began pulling her out of the tree, towards him, and she had to go, had to follow, because she could no longer bear to see the terrible anguish on his face.

But even as Simone started to move, a hand

grabbed her and held on tightly. 'I've got her!' André shouted. 'She's safe.'

Under the tree Cassis was barking, and there were shapes that Simone recognized as Grand-mère and Monsieur Arragon. She hadn't a clue how long they had been there.

Slowly Simone let André help her down the trunk of the tree. She felt dizzy. 'I'm . . . I'm not sure how I got up there,' she said, in answer to Grand-mère's questions.

'Sleepwalking,' Monsieur Arragon murmured.

'It's lucky Cassis woke me up,' André said. 'You must have been dreaming, because you didn't even hear the commotion. Cassis made such a fuss that we all went outside to see what was going on, and there you were, about to fall out of the tree.'

Safe on the ground, Simone was silent and tremulous, unable to believe she had been asleep. She had been saved this time, but she was sure her father would not give up. She knew, now, that she had been wrong about Mum and Billy, that they *did* want her, but she also knew that Jean-Claude wanted her for himself. He did not want to share her with an English stranger, a man called Billy, whom Simone's mother now loved.

'I want to go home,' Simone said tearfully. 'Please, can I go home?'

She meant England, but they all thought she meant she wanted to go into the house.

'Of course, my little one,' Grand-mère said, her face white and strained. 'You're shaking; here, hold on to me.'

Simone felt very wobbly and faint. 'I think she has a fever,' Grand-mère murmured. 'The child is not well at all.'

Grand-mère put Simone straight to bed with a hot

water bottle, for she was shivering uncontrollably. 'Sleep, now,' Grand-mère said.

Simone slept. Luckily, she did not dream.

The doctor came next morning, for Simone had a high temperature. He said she had a virus and must remain in bed and drink plenty of bottled water. He left some tablets for her to take.

Annie and Nicole, back from holiday with their parents, cycled up. They were mad with excitement because that morning Annie's mum had seen an article in the West France newspaper about André and Simone's adventure in the forest. There were two large photographs, one of André and Simone, and the other of all four of them.

'You're famous,' Annie cried, waving the paper in front of Simone's flushed face and knocking over the bottle of tablets on the bedside table.

'Annie, will you stop flapping that newspaper in Simone's face and calm down?' Nicole said, grabbing the paper. 'It says here how brave you and André were, Simone. It tells all about your French father and your English mother, too, and how you are in Brittany for the first time,' she went on.

But Simone was too ill to care. All she wanted was to be left alone, to sleep.

Two days later, she was still not any better. Grand-mère, great shadows under her eyes, called the doctor again.

The doctor seemed concerned. 'I will change the antibiotics,' he murmured to Grand-mère. 'If it doesn't help, we will have to take her into hospital.'

The antibiotics were changed. André came over two or three times a day but Simone barely recognized him. Grand-mère never left her side. Simone was aware that she was there all night, without a break. In her feverish state she was glad. The dreams had come back again, of Jean-Claude calling her, urging her to follow him.

'You must choose, my daughter,' he cried to Simone over and over as she tossed and turned on the bed. Every time she opened her dry, aching eyes, his face looked out at her from the mirror, through the shuttered window, in the image of the wood carving which was no longer Merlin the magician but Jean-Claude. His face looked ravaged with pain and distress. 'You must choose between me and the stranger, Simone. You are all I have, my daughter. All I have left.'

Simone didn't want to choose. She tossed and turned fitfully, too weak to do anything. She didn't want to die, and join Jean-Claude, but she didn't want to reject her father either. 'Stay with me, Simone,' he pleaded. 'Stay with me forever, don't leave me.'

Many times she felt as if she were obeying his will, as she succumbed to the fever and weakness. She felt her life ebbing away, becoming part of the spirit world, part of Jean-Claude's world.

But each time she almost succumbed, the solid, sturdy figure of Billy appeared, saying, 'Come with *us*, Simone. Come with your mum and me, back to England, to our new life there. We love you, Simone. You will be my daughter too, now.'

Jean-Claude, in the mirror, from the eyes of the wood carving, wept and cried out to her again to hurry, he was waiting for her, waiting, waiting . . .

Her fever raged, and she grew weaker. Her only

strength was in the hand that clung to Grand-mère's hand, day and night. She knew that Grand-mère needed her, would never let her go, not even to Jean-Claude, her own son.

Soon it was Grand-mère's face, not her father's, not Billy's, that she saw in her dreams every night. Grand-mère urging her to get well, to live.

'But my father wants me!' she cried out aloud, startling Grand-mère who was as usual sitting at her bedside, soothing her feverish brow with cold compresses.

'Hush, *ma petite*,' Grand-mère whispered. 'You are dreaming.'

Simone was trembling. 'I'm not. Jean-Claude keeps calling me, Grand-mère. He wants me to join him.'

Her voice trailed off, too weak to continue.

Grand-mère was shocked, but she said calmly, 'Hush, Grand-daughter. It is the sickness, making you confused. Your father wants you to live, so that he can live in you.'

'It's Billy,' Simone groaned. 'He's jealous of Billy.'

Grand-mère sighed, and pressed Simone's hand hard with her own calloused one. 'It is the fever confusing you. And your own fears, Simone. In your own heart there must have been seeds of jealousy, it is only natural. Your mother and you have been alone together for so long.'

Simone looked at Grand-mère, her head more clear than it had been for days. 'But Billy . . . he is replacing your own son.'

'My son is dead, little one,' Grand-mère said gently. 'And my grand-daughter is alive. If Billy can be a father to you now, I rejoice, and in my heart I am sure Jean-Claude would rejoice too.'

Simone loosened her grip on Grand-mère's hand.

She had been clutching at it so tightly that there were red marks on the old, papery flesh. She turned her eyes from Grand-mère's wrinkled face on to the mirror, which now seemed to be reflecting nothing but the sunlight which was streaming in from the unshuttered window.

Simone's tired gaze moved to the shelf by the bed and the wooden statue of Merlin, now nothing more than a childish wood carving made by a young boy. Simone looked once again at the mirror. A sudden dazzling beam of light flashed on it like a shooting star, magical and mystical, momentarily blinding her. In the explosion of light she saw Jean-Claude, her father, arms outstretched and reaching out for her. With a cry of joy she ran into his arms and he held her lovingly, joyfully, as she held him. They stood this way for either seconds or for eternity – it seemed like both to Simone, later – until finally they let each other go and Simone drifted into a peaceful, dreamless sleep.

Grand-mère, recognizing that the fever had broken, stayed at her side, and wept tears of relief.

Nine

*T*HE SUN WAS STREAMING THROUGH THE OPEN shutters when Simone opened her eyes again. She thought she was dreaming, for instead of Grand-mère holding her hand, there was Mum.

'Simone? My poor girl, how are you are?' Mum was hugging and kissing her.

Simone was still confused. 'Where's Grand-mère?' she stammered. 'Is Grand-mère all right?'

'Yes, she's exhausted, but fine. She didn't want to leave your bedside, but she looked so drawn and pale I sent her to her room, to sleep. I don't think she's slept since you were taken ill.'

Simone tried to sit up. She was feeling much less dizzy now, and not so hot and feverish. But she was still very weak.

Mum helped prop her up on some pillows. Simone could see the willow tree again, and sure enough, the blackbird was perched on the highest branch, singing away. In the distance, through the open window, she could hear André calling to Cassis.

The door of the bedroom opened and Billy came in, with a tray. There was a small glass of peach juice on the tray, and a bowl of sweetpeas. There was also some fresh bread, butter, jam, cheese.

Billy put down the tray and gave Simone a hearty

hug. 'Your grandmother is fussing around down-stairs, saying you should eat now that your fever has gone down.'

'I sent her to bed!' Mum exclaimed, as if Grand-mère were a child.

'Can I see her, please?' Simone asked.

Grand-mère was fetched, and she was so happy to see Simone sitting up that her tired face instantly became animated. She fussed over Simone, plumped up her pillows, tried to get her to eat a bit of bread and butter.

Finally, satisfied that Simone was really and truly better, she left the room, saying that perhaps now she *would* rest for a bit, and leave Simone alone with her mum and Billy.

'When did you get here?' Simone asked. 'You weren't due back for another week.'

'You won't believe this, but we saw your photo in a newspaper,' Mum said. 'One of the papers in our area had picked up the story from the West France daily. I immediately rang up Annie's mother, to make sure you had all recovered after that ordeal.'

Billy went on with the story. 'Annie's mother told us you were ill. So we packed up and drove all night. We arrived here a couple of hours ago.'

'Was I *that* ill?' Simone murmured.

Mum brushed the hair from Simone's face. 'Well, Annie's mum told us not to worry, but I couldn't bear being so far away from you, knowing you weren't well.'

Billy grinned. 'It was a good excuse, really. Your mother was missing you so much she was dying to get back to Brittany.'

Simone lay back on the pillows and closed her eyes. 'I'm sorry I spoilt your holiday,' she murmured.

'You didn't do anything of the sort,' Billy said firmly. Mum nodded her head in agreement and Billy continued, 'We were both missing you. And we thought it would be a good idea for me to spend more than a night or two here. I've heard so much about Grand-mère, I'd like to get to know her before we go back to England.'

Simone was getting drowsy again. All the excitement of the reunion had tired her.

Mum kissed her, and closed the shutters. Billy said that she ought to rest now, and left the room, saying he'd see her later. As Simone drifted and dozed, she was aware of Mum sitting at her side, holding her hand just as Grand-mère had done during those long, feverish days and nights.

Simone's health improved rapidly, much to everyone's relief.

'Just in time, too,' the doctor said. 'I was about to have her taken into hospital. It was a nasty bug, that. I was worried; I was afraid that it was developing into something worse.'

Grand-mère still looked drawn and exhausted, her skin pale, crumpled like tissue paper. But she was joyous and lighthearted, singing her old Breton songs in the kitchen as she prepared galettes, and crêpes, and gâteaux, and all sorts of wonderful things to whet Simone's appetite.

Simone told Mum about Grand-mère's pains in her chest, and Mum had a word with the doctor when he came the last time to see Simone.

'There's nothing wrong with me,' Grand-mère insisted as the doctor said he wanted to give her a check-up. 'I'm old. All old people have pains. It's nothing.'

But the doctor declared that Grand-mère had something called angina, which was causing the terrible pains in her heart.

'It is not uncommon,' the doctor reassured her. 'You can still lead a perfectly normal life. Luckily, there are tablets I can give you to control it.'

Grand-mère agreed to take the tablets. Later, Simone heard her talking to Mum. Grand-mère was relieved to know at last what it was, for the pains had been excruciating at times. And she was glad that something could be done for it.

André came over often when Simone was convalescing. The doctor made sure she stayed in bed a few days longer, and did not overdo it. Simone felt very weak, so she was happy to obey.

André and Simone played cards, and André read her a story that he had written down for her when she was ill. It was much more real than any of his other stories, with his own made-up characters rather than those of King Arthur and his court. Simone liked it, especially as the main characters were very much like her and André.

'See, you *can* write!' Simone cried. 'It's a good story.'

André was pleased, and shyly showed it to both Nicole and Annie when they came over. Annie, who loved reading, said it was brilliant, and even Nicole, who didn't much, said it was pretty good. 'You must show it to one of the teachers when school starts again,' Nicole suggested.

Mum spent a lot of time with Simone, playing games with her, and just talking.

'Billy is getting on so well with Grand-mère,' Mum said one overcast afternoon. 'He has taken her to Pontivy, to choose some tiles for the bathroom. He's offered to replace all those ones that have fallen off, and redo the bathroom.'

'I thought she'd mind,' Simone said slowly. 'About you and Billy. But she doesn't.'

Mum nodded. 'Not at all. We want her to come to the wedding, you know. She says she couldn't possibly leave Brittany, not even for a week-end. Not at her age.'

'She'd love it once she got there.'

'I know.' Mum looked thoughtful. 'Billy said he'd come and collect her a few days beforehand. That might persuade her.'

'She's family, Mum,' Simone said. 'She's got to be there.'

Mum looked fondly at Simone. 'We'll see what we can do. Between you and André, you got Grand-mère to go further than she's been for years. Maybe she'll attempt England next.'

Grand-mère let Simone choose whatever she wanted of Jean-Claude's, to take back to England. She took the Dominoes set that she and André played with, and several of his books.

'Why don't *you* have the posters?' she suggested to André as they sat in the attic, going through some of the things. 'Grand-mère said you could have anything of my father's that I didn't want. She says they are no good to anyone in the attic.'

They were looking at the poster of the map of

Brittany telling the whole King Arthur story. 'I'll have the others, if you like,' André said. 'But you must have this one.'

They had spread it out on the uneven floor. There was the forest, with Merlin's Tomb, and the Valley of No Return. There were all the figures of the Knights of the Round Table, and the Ladies, and the witches and magicians and sorcerers.

'Yes,' Simone agreed. 'I'd like this one. I'd like to hang it in my bedroom in England.'

André and Simone were quiet for a few moments, looking at the poster and remembering their own adventures. The memories no longer held any terror for Simone.

'I'm going to hang *all* of these up in my bedroom,' André said, finally, indicating the rest of the posters.

'To remind you to take a map and a compass if you ever go into a forest again?' Simone asked teasingly.

André hesitated before replying. 'No,' he said finally. 'To remind me of you.'

There was one more item of Jean-Claude's that Simone took back to England. Packing her suitcases, she left the wood carving until last. She wanted it because it was something her father had made with his own hands, and she knew she would treasure it as long as she lived.

'You're breaking Vivian's spell,' André teased, sitting on her bed as he watched her pack. 'You're rescuing Merlin from the magic the sorceress cast over him in the forest of Brociliande, dooming him to stay there forever.'

Simone smiled, and so did André. 'You ought to be

a writer one day,' Simone said. 'You've got the most vivid imagination of anybody I know.'

The ferry for England was leaving at 11.30 that evening. Grand-mère had invited Nicole and Annie, and André and Monsieur Arragon, for an early supper of crêpes and cider. Billy, Mum and Simone had to leave by eight o'clock.

The two cars were packed and ready to go. Mum and Billy didn't have any cider because they were driving, but Simone was allowed a small glass, and so were the others.

André was very subdued. At one point, after they had eaten, he disappeared. Simone went out looking for him and found him in the apple tree, even though it was stormy again and looked as if it were about to hose down.

'You're not being very friendly,' Simone said.

'You've got Nicole and Annie and everyone,' André said sulkily. 'You don't need me.'

'You're being a baby again,' Simone said. 'I thought you had grown out of all that.'

There was a silence for several minutes. Then there was a rustle of branches and André jumped down from the tree. 'I have,' he said, more cheerily.

'Good. We'd better go back in then.'

They started to walk towards the house.

'Simone,' André said, stopping her before they left the garden. 'You *will* come back, won't you?'

'I've told you a dozen times I will. I can't just abandon Grand-mère, you know.'

André made a monkey face at her. 'What about *me*? You can't just abandon me either.'

Simone laughed. 'As I said, I'll be back. And

— 121 —

anyway, you're coming to visit England. Mum has talked about it to your grandpa, as you know.'

André looked worried. 'Will I like England, Simone? My English is dreadful.'

'You'll have to practise in school, and with Nicole and Annie. I've taught you lots of words already, since I've been here. You'll be fine.'

'What will your friends think of me?'

Simone gave him a playful shove. 'It depends. If you act sensibly, like you *can*, they'll like you fine.'

André grimaced, but then said he'd try. Before they reached the house, he muttered, 'I heard your mother say that Annie and Nicole must come over, too.'

'And why not?' Simone asked. 'They are my friends, too. You're not getting jealous again, are you?'

André rolled his eyes. 'Me, jealous? Never! Anyway, they're *my* friends now, just as much as yours.'

With that, he ran into the house, Simone following close behind him.

It was drizzling rain when the two cars pulled away from Truez-er Lann. All the French people – family and friends – stood at the top of the little lane waving them off, while Cassis ran after the car for a few metres, barking madly.

'*Au revoir, au revoir*,' everyone shouted, until the cars were out of sight. Grand-mère waved a lacy white handkerchief until Monsieur Arragon gently took her hand and walked her into the house.

'*Au revoir*,' Simone called through the open window, though she knew they couldn't hear her anymore. She felt hollow and sad, remembering Grand-mère's waving handkerchief, and André jumping up and down to get his last glimpse of the departing cars.

For all the promises to visit each other, England felt like a very long way away. Grand-mère was old, and with a heart condition. What would the winter be like, for her, especially now, especially when she had got used to having Simone and Mum around?

And André. How many times had he watched his mum and dad drive away down that same road, promising to return soon but never keeping their promise? Simone sighed. The winter would be hard for André too, despite his new friendship with Nicole and Annie. He was still isolated, far from the village, far from his parents.

Mum, hearing Simone's sigh, began to talk. 'It's a nice expression, that one,' she said, not taking her eyes off the road. '*Au revoir.* The French have two words for good-bye. One is *adieu*, which is more final, and the other is *au revoir*, which means good-bye for a time, not forever.'

Simone nodded and stared at the countryside around her. They were driving through a deep valley, around a curving road, and the trees grew thick and green along the sloping hillsides.

Tonight, she would sleep on the ferry, and when she woke, they would be in England. She suddenly longed to see Angie, and their house, and her own bedroom with the red duvet on the bed and her own posters of dolphins on the walls.

'*Au revoir*, France,' she whispered to the passing Brittany countryside, to the acres of sweetcorn about to be harvested, to the gentle hills and the green woodlands.

She looked out at the road ahead and saw it straighten in front of them, on the way to Roscoff and the ferry, and from there home to England.

But she kept thinking of another road, and a small

elfin figure standing on the verge, patiently waiting for someone who never came.

'*Au revoir*, André,' she said aloud. She fixed her eyes firmly on the road ahead of her, and tried not to see the figure become smaller and smaller as the miles stretched between them.